SAFETY NET

Mary Lee Tinney

PublishAmerica
Baltimore

© 2005 by Mary Lee Tinney.

All rights reserved. No part of this book may be reproduced, stored in a retrieval system or transmitted in any form or by any means without the prior written permission of the publishers, except by a reviewer who may quote brief passages in a review to be printed in a newspaper, magazine or journal.

First printing

ISBN: 1-4137-8541-7
PUBLISHED BY PUBLISHAMERICA, LLLP
www.publishamerica.com
Baltimore

Printed in the United States of America

*In memory of my sister, Rachel.
She would have been so proud of me for following my dream.*

Acknowledgments

Thanks to PublishAmerica for giving me the opportunity to see my work in print. To my son-in-law, Mark, who brought me my first computer to get the book "out of my head" and onto paper, and to my daughter, Paula, who came to my aid when the computer threw me curves, my grateful appreciation. And, to all my family and friends, thank you for the encouragement you have given me all these years.

Chapter 1

May 1955

It was Friday...end of the work week. Marcie Capolloni was making her way to the time clock. Marcie was a slight young lady and with her curly brown hair pulled back in a pony tail she appeared hardly more than a teenager. Suddenly a shrill whistle grated on her ears. A slight smile played on her lips. She knew who it was before she heard, "Hey, wait up, Marcie." She slowed her step and looked around . Jeff Martin was loping down the causeway to catch up with her. Jeff had only been working at the Eagle Clothespin Factory here in Shelbyville for a couple weeks, but he had begun paying special attention to her from the first time he saw her.

"What's the big hurry?" he asked as he caught up with her. His blue work shirt and trousers were a bit rumpled and his light brown hair slightly mussed, but his bright blue eyes sparkled as he threw his arm companionably across her shoulders. "I thought it might be fun if we picked up Kev and took in a movie or went bowling or something tonight. How about it?" He shook her shoulder playfully as he asked.

Marcie really enjoyed his company but she had so much to do at home. Also, tomorrow would be two years since she and Kevin had started their "new life." *SHE* had said, "*In two years we will come for you both.*" Marcie couldn't help but be too distracted, wondering what might happen tomorrow, to be any fun tonight. So, she begged off, claiming too many chores at home so as not to hurt his feelings or have him start asking questions that she *must* not answer. But Jeff was not to be put off easily. "OK," he said, "but tomorrow is supposed to be a beautiful day. I'll be by about 11:00 and we're all going on a picnic at the park. My treat! Tell Kev to bring his baseball glove and I'll pitch him a few." With a wave of his hand he took off for the parking lot, giving Marcie no chance to make an excuse.

Chapter 2

Just as predicted, Saturday morning began as a beautiful day, balmy, with the temperature in the mid 70s. Promptly at 11:00 a.m. Jeff's car pulled up out front. Kev, a lively six-year-old boy with curly brown hair was all ready to go, dressed in a favorite pair of dungarees, red tee shirt and red canvas shoes. He loved the attention he received from Jeff. Last night, when Marcie had told him the plans for today, he jumped up and down excitedly, clapping his hands, and had gone immediately to search for his baseball glove. Now he was at the door before Jeff had reached the front porch, and was expressing his eagerness to be on his way. Jeff was relaxed looking in tan trousers and a blue tee shirt. He grabbed Kev and threw him over his shoulder playfully, then set him back down to tussle the curls on his head. At the same time he had his eyes on Marcie who, again, had her hair pulled back in a pony tail with a yellow ribbon tied around it. She was dressed in plaid bermuda shorts with a yellow cotton shirt. *She has no idea how beautiful she is*, thought Jeff, and he felt a tightening in his chest as he looked at her. *Back off*, he said to himself, *you're getting way out of line with these feelings. Nothing can come of it.* But, it was easy to tell oneself that some things were not meant to be — harder, though, to ignore. Shaking the thoughts from his mind, he asked, "Everybody ready? I got fried chicken, potato salad, and apple pie in the cooler. Let's get on our way!"

They found a picnic table under a tree that was just beginning to bud out in its summer leaves. It was a pretty spot for a picnic. Jeff and Kev grabbed the baseball and gloves and ran down the slope to a level spot where they proceeded to pitch and catch and generally have fun. Marcie spread out the food, then called the fellows to come join her before she ate it all. Jeff's landlady had made the picnic lunch for him. It was delicious. She had also tossed in a blanket, which they spread on the ground, and Marcie just wanted to lie down and sleep. The night before had not been restful.

Kev began to grumble. He wanted Jeff to go back down the field and play ball some more. Marcie knew Jeff wanted to relax soon after eating, so she told Kev in no uncertain terms that he could find something else to do for a while. At this time, Kev whirled on Marcie, yelling, "You can't tell me what to do! You're not my—" Marcie clamped her hand over his mouth quickly to prevent him from saying anything further. Kev immediately jerked free from her grasp and took off running down the hill and was soon lost to sight among the other people at the park on this beautiful day. Marcie looked stunned then burst into loud sobs, crumpling to the ground.

Jeff dropped to his knees and brought the sobbing girl to his chest, murmuring, "Don't be so upset, Marcie, I'll go get Kev." He knew this outburst came from more than a kid mouthing off. Patting her back, he spoke in soothing tones, "What is wrong, Marcie? If you can share it with me maybe I can help." But she just shook her head. Finally, Jeff handed her a wad of paper napkins and she wiped her eyes and face.

"I'm sorry to spoil things today, Jeff. If you can go find Kev I think we'd best go home."

Upon arriving at the house, a subdued but still sulking Kev sat in the back seat, in no hurry to get out of the car. A couple of old derelict-looking men were walking down the street placing paper ads in the mailboxes. Marcie went over to collect her mail. As she glanced through the mail, the paper ad fell open and inserted within the fold was a copy of an old newspaper. The headlines glared: LOCAL HOME DESTROYED IN BLAST. CHILDREN MISSING. Marcie gasped and quickly closed the papers together. She looked up and down the street, but there was no sight of the old men who had been placing the papers in the boxes. Jeff noticed that she had suddenly paled. Making a quick decision, he told Marcie he was taking Kev bowling. Not to reward him for his behavior, but to give her a little time to herself to relax and rest. Marcie just nodded her compliance and walked quickly into the house.

Chapter 3

Marcie lay back on her bed with the newspaper copy in her hands, her thoughts going back to two years before. Marcie, then sixteen and a high school junior, had just come in from school when Lisa, her stepmother, called out asking her to accompany her to the shopping center. Marcie knew it was useless to object, so she jumped in the car with Lisa. Upon arriving at the shopping center parking lot, Lisa said, "Come over here for a minute, Marcie. I need to talk to you about something important." They sat down on one of the courtesy benches along the store fronts and Lisa looked at Marcie for a long moment and then began an unbelievable tale. "I can't have this discussion with you in our home because your father and I have reason to believe that the house has been 'bugged' and our conversations are being monitored. For quite sometime now, your father and I have been involved with a business group, which shall remain nameless. Your father has been handling their finances.

"Recently, however, they have been implying that we have been taking some of their money. It may be necessary for us to go into hiding for a while," she said. "Unfortunately, it would be very difficult for us to disappear with two youngsters along. When we return home I am going to show you a briefcase in my bedroom closet. In this briefcase you will find some documents: a social security card and driver's license for you and a birth certificate for Kevin showing you as his mother. Also, a sum of money is stored there. You are to use this money prudently. Never let anyone, not even Kevin, know about it. We have to go to Pittsburgh tomorrow for a few days and Mrs. West will be coming in to stay with you and Kevin. My cue to you that we will be forced into hiding and the plan is to go into effect, will be a phone call saying, 'We will be home tonight by eleven so go ahead and tell Mrs. West to go home.' It is extremely important that you follow these instructions to the letter, especially about Mrs. West leaving." With this, Lisa laid out her plans of deception that would change Marcie and Kevin's lives.

Chapter 4

Three days had passed with no messages from Marcie and Kevin's parents. On Tuesday afternoon Marcie returned from school. Mrs. West had dinner prepared and Kevin was in the den watching cartoons on television. Marcie was preparing to set the table for them to eat when the phone rang. Marcie hesitated before picking up the receiver. She had a sinking feeling that this would be the call she had been dreading. "Hello," she said.

"Hi, Marcie, this is Mom. Just wanted you to know that Dad and I will be coming home tonight. We should get there by 11:00 p.m. or earlier. So tell Mrs. West to go on home. You can look out for Kevin for us until we arrive." Marcie paled and turned to face away from Mrs. West as the call from Lisa was completed. She then relayed the message to Mrs. West that it was okay for her to go home that evening.

Mrs. West stayed to clean up the kitchen after dinner. Then, reassuring Marcie that she would be glad to return later if their parents didn't make it home, she left. Kevin was on the sofa reading his books. Marcie left him there with the admonition that she was straightening up the house some before Mom and Dad returned and would get him ready for bed later.

Marcie went into the attached garage and, climbing onto a step ladder from nearby, she turned the light bulbs so they would not light up when the garage doors opened. Going back into the house, she went upstairs to her parents' bedroom. In the spare closet sat two suitcases already packed for herself and Kevin. These she carried downstairs and placed in the trunk of the family car. She returned and picked up the briefcase Lisa had discussed and carried it down to the garage. Instead of placing the briefcase in the trunk immediately, she opened it and removed the driver's license and social security card in the name of Marcie Capolloni. At the same time, she removed four 50-dollar bills and placed the money in her purse. She then put the briefcase in the trunk of the car and closed it. Upon returning to the kitchen, she proceeded to empty her purse of all her personal credentials. These she put in an envelope to take to her room. Carrying her purse, she went upstairs, this time to her room. She wanted so badly to collect pictures of her family and friends but this was one thing Lisa had warned she must not do. On the shelf in her bedroom closet she removed a box. From it she took a complete change of clothing that Lisa had provided. Removing all her own clothes, she donned a pair of dark blue slacks and a white blouse. She then slipped her feet into a pair of black sandals. Next, she picked up a wig of shoulder length, light brown hair. Pinning her long hair firmly on top of her head. she put on the wig. Next she brushed her eyelashes with just a bit of mascara and then added a touch of rouge to her cheeks. When she had finished, she observed herself in the mirror and was amazed at how natural the wig looked and how much older she appeared.

    It was now getting close to 10:00 p.m. She remembered Lisa's warning: "Be out of the house before 11:00 p.m." Marcie went back downstairs. Kevin, still in his play clothes, had fallen asleep on the sofa. *This will make it easier*, thought Marcie. She did a double check throughout the house to make sure nothing was forgotten. She picked up sweaters for both Kevin and herself and took them out to the car, leaving the front door of the car open. She then returned to the den and, with effort, picked up the sleeping Kevin and carried him out, placing him on the seat of the car and covering him with his sweater. With a feeling of near panic for what the future might hold, she took a deep breath and bravely returned to the kitchen, picked up her purse and the car keys. Not wanting to arouse the neighbors, Marcie opened the garage door as quietly as possible. Putting the car into gear, she allowed it to drift out of the garage and down the driveway. Only then did she start the engine and turn on the lights. Marceline and Kevin Kallinski no longer existed.

Chapter 5

It was a clear night. Stars were thick in the sky. They were on their way to Batesville, the next town, and had been on the road for about twenty minutes when Kevin began to stir. He raised up and, looking around, asked, "Where are we going, Marcie? It's still dark outside." Thus, began the first of many untruths Marcie would have to tell her little half-brother.

"Well, Kev, while you were sleeping, Mom called again and said their plans had changed and we were to go meet her and Dad. We can only drive to Batesville, then we're going to catch a bus. It will be fun! Like an adventure!"

Entering the town of Batesville, Marcie took the route Lisa had given her and parked the car on a side street around the block from the bus station. It was almost midnight and the night had turned a bit chilly. Marcie put Kevin's sweater on him and, donning her own sweater, they got out of the car. She unlocked the trunk of the car and removed the two suitcases and the briefcase. When she closed the car trunk, she left the keys hanging in the lock. "Can you carry this smaller suitcase, Kev?" asked Marcie. "I can manage the other two." They picked up the cases and, without a backward glance, walked toward the lighted bus station.

When they entered the bus station, Kevin noticed Marcie's wig. "What are you doing with that hair on your head?" He giggled. "You look like it's Halloween!" and he began to laugh. Marcie joined him. It was either laugh or cry and she couldn't allow herself that luxury.

    She purchased tickets for the two of them to Muncie, Indiana, and was told the bus would be boarding in fifteen minutes. At about the same time the bus was leaving the station, a group of "punks" were meandering down a street and spotted a parked car with the keys hanging in the trunk. Within minutes they had piled in the car and proceeded to go for a joy ride. The car was later found abandoned along the highway on the other side of town where it had run out of gas.

Chapter 6

It was about 3:00 a.m. Marcie woke when she felt the bus stopping. The driver announced to any passengers who awakened that they were in Greensburg and there would be a twenty-minute rest stop. They were informed that they could get off and get food or drink at the all-night restaurant. Marcie looked out the bus window and saw that the restaurant was part of a motel. She made a quick decision. Rousing Kevin so he could walk with her, they left the bus, carrying the briefcase. Marcie kept it with her at all times. At the restaurant, she asked the waitress if the motel was open at this time of night and was assured that a desk clerk was on duty. She could get a room by just going through the adjoining door to the desk. "Kevin, it is late and we are both tired. I'm going to get a room in this motel for the night. You sit right here in this booth until I get back. I'm going to get our suitcases off the bus. I'm putting this small suitcase right behind you. Don't let anyone near it. I'll be right back." She found the bus driver and was able to retrieve their suitcases. She asked if they could use their tickets on a later bus coming through tomorrow and he punched the tickets indicating they could be used accordingly.

Kevin was asleep within minutes of being tucked into bed. Marcie was very tired. She set the provided alarm clock for 7:00 a.m. There was much to be done tomorrow.

Chapter 7

When the alarm sounded, Marcie jumped from the bed quickly. Kevin was already stirring. She picked up the phone and ordered breakfast for them both from room service.

As soon as she had finished eating, Marcie turned on the television to a cartoon station and told Kevin he was to stay in the room and watch TV until she returned. "I'll bring you a surprise," she said. "Remember, you're not to open the door for anyone. I have the key and can let myself back in." Dressed in her wig she picked up the DO NOT DISTURB sign and placed it on the outside of the door as she left. Her first stop was at the desk where she asked and was advised that check-out time was at noon. She stated that they would be leaving before then and paid her bill. She returned to the motel room once more. While out front, she had spied a used car lot about a half block away. Taking the briefcase with her into the bathroom, she removed $2,500. Again cautioning Kevin not to open the door, she left the room and made her way to the car lot. She spied an elderly-looking salesman who didn't appear to be too "pushy" and approached him about looking at a certain car that she liked the looks of. She told him that all she could afford to pay for the vehicle was $1,200 tops. The salesman looked at the young girl before him and thought of his granddaughter who lived on the West Coast and that he only knew through occasional pictures sent by her mother. Although it reduced his commission considerably, he helped her purchase the 1950s blue Chevrolet that she had selected. Explaining that she and her son were on their way to Muncie, Indiana, and that she did not yet have an address, he arranged for temporary plates and registration until she arrived at her destination.

Marcie drove the car back to the side parking lot of the motel. She returned to the room once again. This time she removed the wig and combed out her long hair, letting it fall down her back. Leaving once more, she walked in the other direction from the motel where the downtown business district seemed to be located. When she returned, Kevin was in for a surprise. She had stopped at a beauty shop and had her hair cut short. She also had stopped at the local 5 & 10 store and made a few other purchases, including some books and small toys for Kevin. She then went into the bathroom and re-packed the suitcases, including her purchases from the 5 & 10. With all the decisions she was having to make, and the traumatic changes in her life, Marcie realized she was starting her period early. Luckily, among her purchases was an extremely large box of Modess sanitary napkins. Now, it was time to go. Making sure she had all their belongings, Marcie and Kevin left the motel. They made their way down the side stairs to the parking lot where she had parked the new car. When Kevin saw they were preparing to get into this strange car he looked at Marcie with puzzlement. "It's ok, Kev, just another surprise for you. This is our car. I'll try to explain things to you as we travel down the highway." Just before she climbed into the car, Marcie glanced in the alcove where drink machines and a newspaper rack was placed. Walking over to the newspaper rack she stared at the headlines...the paper was from their hometown...LOCAL HOME DESTROYED BY BLAST! CHILDREN MISSING! Quickly, she inserted a coin, retrieved the paper and, hurriedly, jumped in the car. Kev was busy playing with his new toys and paid little attention to Marcie. She scanned the news article, verifying that it was indeed her and Kevin's former home that had been destroyed. They were fugitives...*Oh, my God!* thought Marcie, *how am I going to explain things to Kev. He's just a little kid. How can I make him understand that it may be two years before we see Mom and Dad again.* She knew that it would seem like forever to him. Grimly it occurred to her that whoever was after their parents thought they had returned home and had intended to kill the whole family. She was horrified!

Chapter 8

They had been traveling all day, only stopping for sandwiches at lunch time and once for gas. It was approaching evening and Marcie was tired. Also, Kev was getting irritable having been cooped up in the car all day. She looked up ahead and noticed a large sign indicating that they were nearing the town of Shelbyville, Home of the Eagle Clothes Pin Factory. She decided to stop in Shelbyville for the night.

Once within the city limits, Marcie slowed to the required twenty-five miles per hour speed limit. This allowed her the opportunity to look around for a decent-looking restaurant. Up ahead on the right was a small, white frame building with a sign out front: MAMIE'S DINER. It appeared to have once been a residence that had been converted into an eating establishment. It looked clean and quiet so Marcie decided that she and Kevin would stop there for dinner. Once inside, they took a seat in a booth near the front windows. There were only four other customers and they all looked at Marcie and Kevin with curiosity. After all, this was a comparatively small town and all the regular customers at Mamie's Diner knew almost everyone who stopped in for a meal, so any strangers were given the "once over."

The waitress came to take their order, handing Marcie a menu that was filled with all sorts of home-cooked meals. "Hi," she said, "I'm Sadie. The only waitress around. How can I help you?" Without waiting for a response, she continued, "New in town, aren't you? You all visiting or just passing through?" She didn't seem to be asking just to be nosy, but genuinely interested. Marcie smiled and, after ordering two meatloaf dinners, she stated that they were hoping to stop for the night and asked if there were any motels in the area. "Let me get your orders started," replied Sadie, "I'll be right back." After their dinners were served, she said, "Old Miz Sinclair has a boardin' house over about three blocks. If you want me to, I'll be glad to call and see if she has a room available." Marcie expressed her appreciation and off Sadie went to check on a room for her. Returning in a few minutes, she advised that Mrs. Sinclair had one room vacant and would be glad to rent it tonight. Sadie's friendly helpfulness made Marcie want to weep with gratitude. In fact, tears did well up in her eyes. Sadie noted this and thought to herself, *This young girl needs a friend*. When they were through eating and ready to leave, Sadie had drawn a brief map for Marcie, giving explicit directions to Mrs. Sinclair's place. By this time it was beginning to get dark.

"I had best get there while it is still light so I don't get lost," she said to Sadie. "Thank you again for being so kind and helpful." Within five minutes, she was pulling into the driveway of a huge three-story dwelling with welcoming lights shining out across the porch and short walkway from the parking area. A modest white sign with black lettering read: MRS. SINCLAIR'S ROOMING HOUSE. Kindly old Mrs. Sinclair met her at the door, welcoming them both to her home. She was a round little lady with white hair pulled back in a bun. She wore a print dress with a wrap-around apron. When she smiled, there were tiny wrinkles at the corner of her eyes. Kevin shyly said, "Hello," when she spoke to him. Then, surprising them both, he said, "You look like Mrs. Santa." Both Marcie and Mrs. Sinclair broke into laughter.

"Come along, young man," she said. "You look like someone who needs a good night's sleep and I've got just the bed for you." They went upstairs and down the hall three doors. She opened the door and switched on the lights of a large, airy room. Apparently, after Sadie called she had come up and opened the window allowing the cool fresh air to blow in. A large, cozy bed dominated the room with a single closet for their clothing, a night stand, bureau, and a large brass stand with a live green fern made up the furnishings. Everything was extremely clean. A small attached bath consisted of shower stall, basin and commode. "I'll leave you now," she said. "Breakfast comes with the room and is served downstairs in the dining room between 7:00 and 9:00 a.m. If you sleep later than 9:00, I'm sorry but you'll have to eat out. Goodnight!"

Marcie readied the shower for Kev and after he had finished bathing and was in his pajamas, he crawled in the bed with some of his books. By the time Marcie completed her shower and returned to the room, he was fast asleep. It wasn't long before Marcie, too, was sound asleep.

Chapter 9

Marcie opened her eyes slowly. She had slept well and felt refreshed. For a moment, she had forgotten where she was. Soon it all came swooping back. She bolted upright! Kevin was gone! Jumping from the bed, she rushed to the bathroom, but he wasn't there. Donning her clothes as rapidly as possible, she headed downstairs. The first thing she heard, coming from a room near the front of the house, was Kevin's laughter along with that of Mrs. Sinclair. He had managed to dress himself and there he sat at the dining room table with his plate heaped with scrambled eggs and bacon. He was drinking from a large glass of orange juice. When he saw Marcie, he waved his hand and said, "Come on over, Marcie. Mrs. Sinclair has all kinds of good things to eat. I bet you're as hungry as me." Then he began spooning the eggs into his mouth. Mrs. Sinclair motioned for Marcie to take a chair. She then proceeded to fill a plate for Marcie, including buttered toast and a cup of coffee. Marcie wasn't in the habit of drinking coffee but, adding a little cream, she took a sip and found that it was delicious.

Soon Kevin was finished eating and asked if he could go outside and look around. The front yard was very spacious, but Marcie didn't want him to maybe step on Mrs. Sinclair's flowers or anything, so she told Kev he could go outside but he was to stay on the porch. There was a big swing out there and soon he was contentedly swinging away.

Mrs. Sinclair brought the coffee pot and refilled both her own and Marcie's cups, then sat down. "This is my little rest time," she explained. "Soon I must get up and clean up these dishes, change all the beds, and straighten up the rooms. Then there's laundry to be done. No rest for the wicked, as the saying goes. Guess I must be pretty bad," she chuckled. Marcie smiled and said she didn't believe there was a wicked bone in Mrs. Sinclair's body. After a few minutes of discussion about the weather and such, Marcie asked Mrs. Sinclair if she knew of any employment in Shelbyville. "As a matter of fact," she replied, "I hear tell their adding another shift over at the Clothes Pin Factory. If you want to go check on a job, I'll be happy to look after Kevin for you. He's such a sweet little boy!" She then gave Marcie directions to the factory. Marcie went up to the room and made herself presentable for job hunting. She then went down and explained to Kevin that she was going somewhere for about an hour and that Mrs. Sinclair was going to look out for him until she got back. "You're to stay within her sight and mind what she says, Kev." She had brought some of his toys down and he proceeded to crawl around on the porch playing contentedly.

Chapter 10

Back at Mrs. Sinclair's, Marcie parked the car and jumped out, calling for Kevin, who came running out of the house with a big cookie in his hand. "Guess what, Kev?" she yelled, grabbing him up and swinging him around. "How would you like to live here in Shelbyville? I got a job and a lead on a place to live."

"Well," Kevin asked, "why can't we just stay with Mrs. Sinclair? She likes me and she gives me cookies. They're still warm from the oven. She even let me help her. I stirred the batter." Marcie laughed. They walked hand in hand into the house. Mrs. Sinclair was coming out of the kitchen. "How did it go?" she asked. Marcie told her she was hired and was to start work on Monday. This was Thursday. She had lots to do before Monday.

She asked Mrs. Sinclair if she knew Okey and Della Chidester. "Oh, yes," she replied. "They're two of the nicest people around. How do you know about them?" Marcie then explained that, while interviewing for the job, she asked one of the ladies in the office if they knew of a place for rent and was referred to the Chidesters. It seems that their daughter, who is married to a service man, just left with her children to join him in California. They had been living in a small house next door to her parents and, since it was now vacant, the office girl thought they might want to rent it out.

"Well," Marcie said, it's just a couple of blocks from the

factory so I stopped and talked to them on my way back here. It's a perfect little place. And," she continued, "they might even look after Kevin for me. Isn't that just great? I can't believe how friendly and nice everybody in this town is. I just know we'll do fine staying here! Thank you, Mrs. Sinclair. I've got tons of things to do so I will get on my way." As she and Kevin pulled out of the parking lot, he was waving to Mrs. Sinclair and yelling that they would be back for a visit soon.

The old lady smiled and waved at the retreating car. *What a lovely girl and sweet young boy,* she thought, *I do hope things work out for them and they come visit me often.*

Chapter 11

"Right now, Kevin, we need to have a talk." They took their hot dogs and cartons of milk and found a seat on a bench in the local park. Marcie began to try and explain to the young boy why they were on their own and why Mom and Dad wouldn't be back for a long time…not until he was ready to go to school. The really hard part was getting him to understand that he was to think of her, Marcie, as his Mom instead of his sister. "Until Mom and Dad return, I have to be responsible for you and it will make everything easier if everybody around here thinks you're my kid," she said. "You can still call me Marcie. Anymore, lots of parents let their kids call them by their first name. That way you won't have to keep reminding yourself to say 'Mom' when you speak to me or of me to others." The young boy was getting restless. He didn't really understand any of this. He just wanted to see where they were going to be living and meet the new people Marcie called their "landlords…"whatever that meant.

They pulled into a gravel driveway. On the right was a trim, white ranch house with a picket fence around the front yard. Marcie explained that the Chidesters lived there. "We will be in the little white bungalow over here," she said, pointing to the left of the driveway. It was a small white house with green shutters. Two steps led up to a front porch, which had a swing hanging on it. The lawn was green with new spring grass and you could see where flower beds had been freshly mulched and were ready for new plants to be set in place. Along the side of the porch, a climber rose that had survived the winter had green shoots poking out. Marcie could envision all the beautiful roses and the pleasant scent they would provide all summer.

They heard a door opening at the ranch house. Marcie told Kevin to mind his manners and they got out of the car. Mr. and Mrs. Chidester came across the yard to greet them. Mrs. Chidester stooped down in front of Kevin and patted his cheek. "My, you're a nice big boy for four years," she said. "And just look at those pretty brown eyes." Mr. Chidester grinned at Kevin and said, "I bet he's got a girlfriend, too, he's so handsome."

"Uh uh," said Kevin quickly, "I don't like girls." The Chidesters laughed.

"We have two grandchildren, a girl and a boy. They just moved all the way to California and we miss them something terrible. Maybe you can help us not be so lonely. Think so, Kevin?" asked Mrs. Chidester.

"I'll come over and help you make cookies," he replied. "Mrs. Sinclair let me stir the batter for her cookies. She gave me two of them for helping her. She said I did *real good,* too!" Mrs. Chidester took his small hand, assuring him that she could use someone to help her make cookies, and led the way to the smaller house.

The front door opened directly into the living room. There were polished hardwood floors throughout. Off to the left was a small dining area. The kitchen could be reached from both the dining area and the living room. A central hallway opened off to two bedrooms on the right and the utility room and bathroom on the left at the rear of the house. There was no furniture, but the curtains had been left at the windows. Mrs. Chidester explained that their daughter left the curtains since they probably wouldn't fit any windows at their place in California.

Marcie began making notes of everything she would need to buy. The kitchen had a stove and refrigerator already. She would only need dishes, utensils and dish towels. That left furniture for the dining room and living room, a TV, beds and bureaus and linens and towels for the bathroom. Also, some throw rugs for in front of the beds and the sofa. She turned to Mrs. Chidester and asked her where she thought she could get the best buys on furniture. "Oh, you'll want to go to Cohens on High Street," she answered. "It's not the best quality, but it's good, sturdy furniture for someone starting out."

"What do you think, Kev?" Marcie asked. "Want to live here?"

"Yes!" he yelled. "Me and Mr. Chidester are gonna look for worms and he's gonna take me fishin.'" He tugged on Marcie's hand and pulled her down to him. Whispering, he said, "Mr. Chidester wants me to call him PawPaw. Is that OK? I really like him!" Marcie smiled at the little boy and assured him that would be ok as long as Mr. Chidester asked him to do so. "WOW, it's ok, PawPaw."

Marcie said, "But right now, Kev, we gotta go shopping so we can have a bed to sleep on tonight." With that, Mrs. Chidester handed her the keys to the house and she and Kev climbed in the car for a shopping spree. She worried that she might not have enough money. She had never shopped for furniture before and had no idea of the cost.

At the store, Marcie and Kevin were having great fun making their selections. She found that the store had lots of "giveaways." When she bought a table and four chairs, a set of dishes came with it, free; with the beds and foundations came bedspreads with each, free; with the sofa and end tables, free table lamps. They then picked out an inexpensive television. She decided to also get a washer and dryer. With having to work, she wouldn't be able to run to a laundromat to keep up with the dirty clothes. She explained their need for the items to be delivered that day and was assured that the truck would be there before 6:00 p.m. Next they went to the 5 & 10. She still needed pots and pans, towels, bed linens, and bathroom rugs. They found a "Davy Crockett" rug for Kevin's room and an oval rug in bright colors for her bedroom, plus a nice four-by-eight in muted colors for the living room. Next, a stop to the grocery store was in order. They needed everything from salt, spices, soups, meats, cereal, milk and juice.

They arrived home (it felt so good to think of this place as "home") and had just finished putting the groceries away when the furniture truck rolled up. How exciting it was to have the delivery men place the new items around in the house. Hooking up the washer and dryer took awhile but the men knew what they were doing and soon all was in good working order.

She carried Kevin's suitcase into his room and, laying it on his bed, opened it up. She told Kevin to put his clothes in the bureau drawers. "That way you'll know where your socks and underwear are and won't have to depend on me to find them for you," Marcie said.

Next, she went into her bedroom and proceeded to put away her clothing. On the top shelf of her closet she placed the large Modess box. *That way Kevin won't be asking questions about things that I don't want to have to explain,* she thought to herself.

With the traveling they had done, she already had enough laundry to try out the new washer and dryer…she began to whistle as she worked. There was such a feeling of contentment here.

Chapter 12

Slowly, Marcie's thoughts returned to the present. *What's going to happen now?* she wondered. She and Kevin had come to love it there in Shelbyville. Marcie found she didn't want to go back…Back, there was nothing to go back to…their home was gone. She had no idea where her parents had been these past two years. Her father had been so distant for at least a year before all this had come about, she didn't even feel she knew who he was. She knew that, deep inside, she blamed Lisa for everything that happened. Oh, her father should have stood up to her, but ever since Mama's death he just seemed to have let life drift by. When he met Lisa and they decided to marry, Marcie thought he might become his sweet and caring self again. But that didn't happen. He simply went to work and returned home, allowing Lisa to make all the decisions. He seemed happy enough when Kevin was born, but still maintained his distance from them all. All Marcie knew was that she and Kevin were very happy *here*.

Kevin adored the Chidesters and they thought of him as another grandchild. Della Chidester looked after him while Marcie was at work and PawPaw (even Marcie called him that now) took him fishing and, during the first winter they were there, he got the old sled out of the garage and took Kevin out on the slope in the park to join the other children sledding. And then, this past Christmas Eve, there was a knock on the front door and a "HO! HO! HO!" was heard. Kevin's eyes became huge as he looked at Marcie. "It must be Santa Claus," she said. "Let's go find out!" When they opened the door, there, in a box with a big red bow around her neck was the most adorable little mongrel puppy they had ever seen. A note attached read: TO KEVIN – FOR BEING A GOOD BOY ALL YEAR! Marcie knew Della and PawPaw had done this. Kevin was ecstatic…so was the puppy because she immediately made a puddle on the floor.

Kevin crowed, "We'll name her Puddles." And Puddles had become a part of the family. They still visited Mrs. Sinclair from time to time. Last Christmas, Kevin had made a pinecone ornament for her Christmas tree. When he gave it to her she cried. Even Sadie (her last name was Hawkins, which everyone teased her about, since she was an "old maid") remained a good friend to Marcie. At work, many of the young, single workers included Marcie in their social activities. It was really a contented life she and Kevin shared in Shelbyville.

I must get up and do the laundry, thought Marcie. *Maybe nothing will happen after all.* But she picked up that copy of the old newspaper and knew, without a doubt, something was about to occur that would cause a great upheaval in her and Kevin's lives again. She rolled over putting her face in the pillow, crying, "Why couldn't they just stay gone forever!" She immediately had feelings of shame for such thoughts. Then, shaking her head, she rose from the bed and muttered to herself, "Whatever happens will happen, I have no control over it." With that, she went about gathering the laundry and doing other weekend chores.

Jeff and Kevin returned. Marcie thanked him for taking Kevin for the afternoon. She knew he wanted her to invite him to stay awhile, but she politely ignored his hints and, after a few minutes, he said goodbye and left.

Marcie was putting the final touches to cleaning up the kitchen. Kevin was bathed and ready for bed. He was on the sofa watching TV with Puddles asleep at his side. As Marcie came out of the kitchen into the living room, something caught her eye. Under the front door a red light flashed on and off. Looking closely, she spied a piece of paper half in and half out from under the door. Walking over to the door slowly, so as not to attract Kevin's attention, she stooped and pulled the paper toward her. Written with a black marker, the note read: SAY NOTHING. THE HOUSE IS BUGGED. GO TO THE BACK DOOR, MOTHER IS WAITING. Marcie gasped audibly. Kevin turned and looked at her, but when she said nothing, he turned back to the TV. Moving as though in a dream, Marcie went back into the kitchen. Not turning on the light, she went to the door, unlatched it, and as she reached for the door knob, the door was quickly pushed open and a figure dressed entirely in black garb pushed forward and into the room. The door was just as quickly closed again. It was Lisa. She held her finger across her lips, silently telling Marcie to say nothing. From within her jacket she pulled a small writing pad along with a marking pencil. IT'S TIME TO GO, she wrote. GET KEVIN AND THE BRIEFCASE. Marcie was stunned. There had been no greeting or hug or anything indicating she was glad to have the family back together. Her only interest seemed to be with the briefcase and urgency in leaving. She was writing furiously on the pad, which she handed to Marcie. I'LL LEAVE IT TO YOU TO GET KEVIN WITHOUT HAVING HIM SAY ANYTHING ALOUD...BETTER GET EVERYTHING READY TO GO FIRST...DON'T PACK. JUST GET A JACKET, SOMETHING DARK. LEAVE EVERYTHING ELSE, INCLUDING THE DOG.

That dog, thought Marcie, *some watchdog. She's still sleeping on the sofa*. Retrieving the notepad, Lisa resumed writing: REMEMBER, THE FEDS ARE JUST WAITING TO GRAB US. YOU'LL BE INVOLVED, TOO, BECAUSE OF THE MONEY. SO, DON'T TRY ANYTHING FUNNY. WHAT WILL BECOME OF KEVIN IF ALL OF US ARE IN JAIL? THEY'LL PUT HIM IN ONE OF THOSE FOSTER HOMES. BRING ME THE BRIEFCASE NOW! Marcie couldn't believe her eyes. What was Lisa trying to do. She couldn't believe that Lisa meant to brand her as a criminal, but that was certainly how the note sounded. Marcie's thoughts were in a whirl. What was she to do. If she just started yelling, would the police really come and take Kevin away. No! No, that was unthinkable! Marcie nodded her head and backed out of the kitchen. She went into her bedroom and to the closet. Pulling out the suitcase, she began throwing things into it, then remembered Lisa's admonition to "take nothing." *I will take some things*, she thought defiantly. She placed the large Modess box inside the suitcase along with a "Precious Moments" statuette that Jeff had given her for Easter. She placed the few items of clothing she had selected carefully on top. She then went into Kevin's room and quickly gathered a few items of clothing along with his favorite bear and a few books, which she carried into her room and placed inside the suitcase. As she started toward the living room to get Kevin, Lisa looked at her and began writing furiously: WHERE'S THE BRIEFCASE? Marcie mouthed, "It's gone!" then turned quickly and went to Kevin.

She knelt beside him as he sat on the sofa. Whispering very softly, Marcie said, "Don't say anything, Kevin, we are 'bugged.' Come with me into your room." When they reached the room, still whispering, Marcie told him that Mom was in the kitchen but that he couldn't say a word because Mom and Dad were in trouble and if someone overheard them, the police might come and take them away. Kevin's eyes became larger and darker. He didn't understand much except that Mom was there and if he didn't keep really quiet, he might get her in trouble. Funny, but he couldn't quite remember what his Mom looked like...Marcie was saying they had to sneak out the back door and go with Mom...but he didn't want to go anywhere. He liked it fine just where they were living now...he started to squirm in protest. "Let's go into my room," Marcie whispered. As they entered the hallway, Lisa was in the kitchen door leading into the living room. She held up the writing pad on which she had written: GET THE BRIEFCASE AND COME

NOW! Instead, Marcie pulled Kevin down the hall and into her room, closing the door behind them.

Kneeling down beside Kevin, she put her arms around him and whispered, "What do you want to do, Kev? Do we take the suitcase and go or do we stay here?"

He looked at Marcie and said, "Who is that person in our kitchen? She looks mean. I don't want to go anywhere, 'specially not with her."

"Then help me push the bureau across the door so they can't get to us," she said. Between them, they were able to shove it across the door. Rather loudly, Marcie spoke, "OK, whoever is supposed to be listening, *they* are here. Kev and I will wait five minutes, then we'll have to go with them if you don't show up." With her arms around Kevin's shoulders, they sat down on the foot of her bed to wait. They both jumped at the sudden outburst from the hallway.

"You Bitch!" they heard Lisa scream. Then there was a loud bump on the bedroom door and Marcie knew Lisa was trying to get in. "Give me that briefcase, NOW," she screeched, all the while slamming against the door, attempting to force it open. Marcie pushed Kevin down, telling him to crawl under the bed. Within minutes, all hell broke loose. There was a crash as the front door was forced open. Strange voices were yelling for someone to drop the gun...at that moment, there was the sound of gunshots. Marcie screamed as she felt pain rip through her upper leg. Looking down, she saw blood soaking through the denim of her jeans. Then she fell.

Kevin scampered from under the bed and began screaming, "Marcie, Marcie, you're bleeding! Somebody help Marcie, she's hurt bad!" At this point, he was screaming hysterically. There was so much noise...people all yelling at once...a woman cursing...then, someone was at the bedroom door...pushing against the bureau. It was Jeff's voice, yelling for Kevin to unlock the door. "Jeff, it's not locked...hurry, Marcie's hurt...she's bleeding..." He heard Jeff yelling for someone to give him a hand with the door and, suddenly, the bureau moved enough for Jeff to squeeze through.

He knelt immediately beside Marcie. Grabbing a knife from his pocket, he made a slit in her jeans, exposing the bleeding injury on her thigh. Turning to Kev, he spoke softly, "She's gonna be okay, Kev. I need you to run to the bathroom and bring a bunch of bath towels. Quick!" To others who were entering the room, he said with the voice of authority, "Sam, get an ambulance here, and I want you to take charge of the boy. Don't let anyone near him! You might check with the Chidesters next door; if it's OK with them, take him there, but you stay with him as well." At this time, Kev returned with the towels. "Now, Kev, go wet a washcloth and bring it here so we can put it on Marcie's brow." He ran to do Jeff's bidding. While he was out of the room, Jeff proceeded to place the towels around the wound, attempting to stop the bleeding. Marcie began to rouse with a low moan. Jeff gently placed his arm under her shoulders and turned her face toward him. "Lie still, Marcie," he said, "the ambulance will be here soon."

"Kevin," she muttered, "where's Kevin?"

"He's right here," Jeff replied, as Kevin entered with the wash cloth. His small hands couldn't wring it out very well, and it was drippy. Jeff unobtrusively gave it a squeeze onto Marcie's already ruined jeans then folded it and asked Kev to hold it on her brow. As soon as Marcie saw Kevin she breathed a sigh of relief and Jeff could feel her relax against his arm. With his left hand, he cupped her face and whispered, "Oh, Marcie, I never wanted anyone to get hurt, especially you or Kevin." She looked at him with questions in her eyes, but she was too weak to voice them now. At that moment they heard the wail of sirens. The ambulance would soon be there.

As they began to wheel Marcie from the house, Kevin started crying. He grabbed onto the gurney and wouldn't let go. Finally, Jeff was able to pry his fingers loose. He picked him up into his arms, saying, "It's ok, Kev, they're gonna fix Marcie up so she doesn't hurt anymore. You stay here." With a nod toward Sam who came over to where they stood, he said to Kevin, "This is my good buddy, Sam, he's going to take you over to PawPaw Chidester's house and stay with you until I finish up here. As soon as I'm through, I'll come get you and we'll go to the hospital and see Marcie. I promise it won't be very long. Will you be a big fella, now, and go with Sam?" Kevin had his head buried in Jeff's shoulder, but he looked up at Sam and nodded his agreement. Sam carried the young boy across to the Chidesters, who immediately began fussing over him. They assured Kevin that Marcie was going to be OK. So, with a glass of milk and a cookie he curled up on PawPaw's lap.

Back at the house, Jeff began giving orders. Both John and Lisa Kallinski were in custody. To one of his agents, he said, "The bullet that hit the young girl went completely through her leg. I want it found and the gun that fired it identified. Get on it, will you!"

It was more than an hour later when Jeff appeared at the Chidester's front door, asking about Kevin. Mrs. Chidester said, "The poor little tyke is being very brave, but he's worried sick about Marcie, as we all are. Have you any news of her?" she asked.

"No," replied Jeff, "but, I'm going to take Kevin with me and we're heading for the hospital right now. If you all," indicating both Mr. and Mrs Chidester, "want to come along, you're welcome. It might be good if you do, that way, as soon as Kevin is assured that Marcie's going to be alright, maybe he'll come back here with you all and get some sleep. Sam will go along and he can bring you back. If it's alright with you, I'd like him to spend the night here just to make sure no one bothers you all." The Chidesters nodded their consent and went immediately to get their jackets as well as a sweater for Kevin.

Soon, they were being shown into the hospital room where Marcie lay sleeping. Kevin went immediately to her. Jeff picked him up and set him on the bed next to her, making sure it was on her uninjured side. Slowly, she opened her eyes. It was difficult to focus, but she felt Kevin's small hand patting hers. She turned in his direction, and he threw his arms around her neck, sobbing. "I was so scared, Marcie, so scared," he cried. She patted his back gently and a silent tear slid down the side of her face and into the pillow. PawPaw leaned down and gave her a peck on the cheek. He then picked up Kevin and walked out of the room with him. Mrs. Chidester took her hand, asking how she felt.

"Groggy," she whispered, "but, I don't hurt."

"Well, dear, you go to sleep now. Kevin will be with us until you're able to come home. Everything is going to be alright. Don't you fret about a thing!" With that, she gave Marcie's cheek a pat and she, too, left the room. Sam would be taking them and Kevin back home.

Jeff stood beside her bed. He then pulled a chair up close and sat down looking into her face. He picked up her hand and brought it to his lips. At that point, he bowed his head and his shoulders began to shake. His tears were warm against her fingers. She had so many questions to ask, but for now she just wanted to sleep, and it felt so good to have Jeff holding her hand. Why was he crying, though?...Then, she slept.

Chapter 13

Marcie had been in the hospital for three days. Each day, Jeff dropped by to visit her. He always brought Kevin with him. In the evenings, however, he came alone, bringing her flowers and staying to talk. Gradually the story unfolded. Jeff was an agent with the FBI. It had taken them almost the full two years to locate her and Kevin. "You're pretty good at losing yourself," he told her. Today, though, she was going home. Jeff promised to pick her up. She heard his voice in the hall. He knew all the nurses on the floor and was chatting away with them. Then he appeared in her doorway with a shopping bag in hand with some clothes Mrs. Chidester had selected for her to wear home, some underwear and a simple wraparound skirt in print pattern with a pink shirt. She was on crutches and couldn't get trousers on over the bandages around her thigh.

As Marcie dressed, she contemplated her future. As Jeff had explained, Marcie's dad and Lisa had stolen money from the mob they had become affiliated with. For the past two years they had been on the run from both the mob and the FBI. Jeff told her that her parents were being held without bond and that a trial was scheduled for next month. There was a question of a missing briefcase that Lisa kept talking about. He asked Marcie if she knew where it could be. "I left it somewhere while we were traveling," she said, "I have no idea where. It's gone! Lost!"

When Marcie returned home, Kevin and the Chidesters were

there to greet her as well as Puddles, who dashed madly around her, barking at the crutches that Marcie needed to get around. She tried to chew on them, but Kevin picked her up so she could give Marcie a "hello" lick on the face. Everyone laughed uproariously at the dog's antics.

Jeff helped Marcie into the house. She was amazed. Thanks to Mrs. Chidester and Sadie, the whole house had been cleaned. PawPaw had even repaired the wall where the bullet that had struck Marcie had crashed through. Jeff didn't tell her—it would come out during the trial of her parents—but the bullet that had passed through Marcie's leg had come from the gun Lisa was carrying.

The management at Eagle Clothes Pin were very understanding and supportive of Marcie. They urged her to use her accumulated sick leave to allow her leg to heal. Within ten days, however, she was back at work. They put her on light duty and she wasn't required to stand at the conveyor belt as she had done before the injury, though. She was lonely, too. Jeff had left town a week ago. He had to report back to Washington, D.C. There was an ache in her heart when she thought about him. She hadn't realized how much she would miss him until he was gone. He hadn't called her, so she surmised that he had a separate life that he was catching up with in D.C. Maybe he was even married. *How very little I actually know about him*, she thought. *All I really know is that I owe him my life. I'll never forget him.* A tear welled up and ran down her cheek as she remembered that night in the hospital when he had cried because she had been hurt.

Chapter 14

Marcie and Kevin were at the courthouse for the trial of John and Lisa. Marcie was no longer using crutches, although she did walk with a bit of a limp. When she was called to testify, she looked at her father, but he only bowed his head and refused to acknowledge her even with a nod. Lisa, on the other hand, glared at her with venom in her eyes. Marcie was devastated. She and Kevin were truly on their own now. The lawyers kept asking her what happened to the briefcase Lisa had given her. She repeatedly told the court that it had been left somewhere during her and Kevin's travels, but she did not remember when or where it was left behind. After her testimony, she and Kev were seated in the gallery when someone tapped her shoulder. Looking around, there was Sam, Jeff's friend. He whispered that Jeff was down the hall and wanted to see them. Marcie grabbed Kevin's hand and they followed Sam.

As they entered one of the vacant court rooms, Kev gave a whoop and ran, leaping into Jeff's outstretched arms. Marcie's face lit up. She, too, wanted to run and throw herself into his arms, but held back. *How foolish of me*, she thought, *he's only here because of the trial.* Then he set Kevin aside and, holding both his arms wide, looked at Marcie and said, "Well, don't I get a hug from you?" Marcie wanted to weep, but instead she smiled widely and rushed to give him a hug. His arms wrapped tightly around her. Then, tilting her face up with a finger under her chin, he looked warmly into her eyes and asked, huskily, how she was doing. His eyes drifted down to her soft lips. Oh, how much he wanted to kiss her! *Mustn't rush things*, he said to himself. Turning to Kevin, he said, "How would you like to go with Sam and get some ice cream?"

"Yeah!" Kev shouted.

"Good!" said Jeff, "because I've got something important to discuss with Marcie. So, you two go across the street and get a cone while we talk. Okay, ol' buddy?" Kevin latched onto Sam's hand and away they went. Marcie looked at Jeff in puzzlement.

As soon as they were alone, Jeff took Marcie's hand and pulled her over to sit alongside him on one of the benches. He first asked about her leg and was assured that it was healing nicely. Then, holding her hand and looking into her troubled eyes, he began, "There's so much to be said, and so little time. To begin with, you and Kevin will not be safe staying here. Those mobsters will be after you." Marcie's eyes widened and she gave a gasp. "I have a solution to your problem, but it is an extremely selfish one on my behalf," he said. He still held her hand and then reached out and pulled her close to his side. "Marcie, I was assigned to this case two years ago. When we located you and Kev at long last, I came to Shelbyville to make contact with you. I was intrigued by the notion that a wisp of girl, at so young an age, could so completely fool the department and I wanted to see for myself what kind of person you were. Little did I know that, from the moment I laid eyes on you, my heart would be lost." Marcie looked at Jeff, her eyes widening. Was he indeed saying what she had been longing to hear? "In other words, Marcie, I'm in love with you. My solution to the whole problem is for us to become engaged now and I'll send you and Kev to Oregon to be with my parents. Sweetheart, I wish this could be done differently. You deserve to be courted…wooed…or whatever the right word is…but, we don't have any time. It is vital that the two of you be on your way as soon as the verdict is in on your parents' trial. I know I'm pushing things with you, but I need to know how you feel. As soon as this trial is over, I must report back to D.C. I have put in for a transfer back to my home state and that usually takes about six months to take effect. If you're agreeable, I can put things in motion immediately." Then, putting both hands on Marcie's shoulders, he pulled her around to face him. "Marcie Kallinski, will you marry me?" he asked. Looking into his blue eyes, Marcie could see the love he had for her.

"OH, yessss!" she cried, throwing her arms around his neck. Only then did he lower his head to those soft lips that he had waited so long to taste. Marcie had never been kissed with so much emotion. She shivered.

Jeff lifted his lips from hers and asked, "Why did you shiver just now?"

"It was with delight," she replied softly, leaning into his arms with her head on his shoulder. After a few moments, Jeff reached into his pocket and brought out a small box.

Handing it to Marcie, he said, "Sweetheart, for security purposes, I have to ask you to keep the ring on a chain around your neck until you arrive in Oregon. But, for now, let's see how it looks on that third finger, left hand." Marcie opened the box and removed a sparkling gold engagement ring with a half carat diamond setting. She handed the ring to Jeff who placed it on her finger. Then she saw that a fine gold chain was included in the box. Jeff ceremoniously kissed her hand with the ring, then slipped it off her finger, threaded it on the chain and placed the chain around her neck. "You've made me the happiest guy in the world, Marcie," said Jeff as he nuzzled her neck.

She put her hands on either side of his face and, looking into his eyes, said, "Jeff, I love you, too, and want to shout it out loud, but I understand the need for secrecy right now. Also, it will be best if we don't mention our plans just yet to Kev. He's confused enough with everything that is happening to us."

"Speaking of Kevin," said Jeff, "the next thing that must be taken care of immediately is his legal custody. I've had an attorney friend of mine draw up the necessary papers for you. A judge is standing by now and we can go down the hall and take care of this." Marcie was in a whirl. She had no idea that there had been any possibility that Kevin might be taken away. Thank God that Jeff knew about these things and was there to guide her.

At this time, Sam and Kev returned and Kev was bubbling over with happiness at his brief outing. He also had ice cream on his face. Marcie got tissues from her purse and cleaned him up as best she could. Jeff briefly explained to Kevin that they had to go talk to a judge about who he should be living with. "Well, I live with Marcie, Jeff, you oughta know that," he said.

"I do know that," said Jeff, laughing," but the judge wants to make everything legal. So let's go down the hall and talk with him, OK?"

"Sure," said Kevin. Grabbing Marcie and Jeff's hands he skipped along the hall between them. Within fifteen minutes, Marcie had legal guardianship of her brother taken care of and the paper tucked away in her purse. She held tightly to Kev's hand and kept a grip on Jeff's arm. After what Jeff had said about the mob, she was afraid to let either of them out of her sight.

The trial continued for two more days. Each night, Jeff came by the house and Marcie made up a bed for him on the sofa. He intended to stay near and protect them both. Each evening, they all three discussed the planned move West to stay with Jeff's parents. But they still did not mention their coming marriage to Kevin. Jeff gave her coded labels, which Marcie had to place on all the pieces of furniture that she wanted to keep. It would be taken into storage as soon as she and Kevin left town, where it would remain until a later date when it could be shipped according to Jeff's instructions. They were busy during this time, packing dishes and linens, preparing them for storage. It was decided they would take only their clothing and a few of Kevin's toys with them when they flew to the West Coast. All the other items would go in storage along with the furniture.

One evening, Jeff said, "The jury will most likely bring in a verdict tomorrow. We must have everything ready for the move immediately after. So, one last thing to cover...Kev, Puddles will have to stay here. I've talked with PawPaw and Della and they want her to live with them. Can you handle that?" Puddles was lying on Kevin's lap and he picked her up and hugged her real tight. Puddles began to squirm and whine. He loosened his hold on her somewhat and looked at Jeff and Marcie with eyes filled with tears. The tears overflowed and soon he was sobbing into the fur of the little dog. Puddles wiggled and tried to lick his face. Marcie went to him and, putting her arms around both Kev and the dog, she, too, began to cry. After a few moments, she got herself under control.

Patting Kevin, she whispered, "I know it's hard to say goodbye to Puddles, but we both know that she'll have a real good home with PawPaw and Della. As a going away present to them, let's give them a camera. That way they can take pictures of Puddles and each other to send us so we can see how everyone is getting along." Jeff felt like the biggest "meanie" alive. He wished there was some way for them to take the little dog. But right now it was impossible. Marcie spoke up. "Let's go to the drug store now and get the camera, Kevin. Then we can take it and Puddles over to the Chidesters. We have to say goodbye to them, too. There may not be any time tomorrow.

Later that night, as they returned to their own home, Marcie and Kevin were both unconsolable. Marcie got Kevin ready for bed and he hugged his teddy bear real tight, saying, "No one can tell me I can't take Teddy."

"Yes, Kev, Teddy goes with you," she said. As the young boy cried himself to sleep, Marcie went about, making sure all his stuff was packed that they intended to take. She was in her own room with a half-filled suitcase open on her bed when Jeff appeared in the doorway. "Marcie," he said, "you know if there was any way at all that this could have been prevented I would have done it. I hate seeing you both hurt so much. Please forgive me!" There were tears in his eyes as he looked at her. Marcie went to him then and they comforted each other. As he held her, he looked around the room that had been stripped of all the personal items that make a home. He glanced at the suitcase and had to stifle a laugh. Inside the suitcase was a large box of Modess. *Just like this naive woman-child,* he thought, *she is too bashful to put so intimate an item in a bag or packing box. Still thinks men don't know about these things.* He wondered, again, if she truly loved him...or was she reacting to the dangerous situation in which she found herself and Kevin, and clinging to the one person she found she could trust to take care of them. If this was true, the six months she would have to herself in Oregon would give her time to realize it. Although he loved her dearly, he would never hold her to a promise made, perhaps, in a moment of panic. With that thought, he kissed her goodnight and went to his bed on the sofa.

The jury filed in and took their seats. The bailiff carried the copy of the verdict to the judge, who asked John and Lisa to rise. He then read: "We, the jury, find the defendants, John and Lisa Kallinski, GUILTY OF RACKETEERING." Jeff had accompanied Marcie and Kevin to the courthouse. They were seated near the front.

As the verdict was read, Lisa turned toward Marcie and screamed, "You'll be sorry, you USELESS, FORGETFUL, LYING BITCH! I won't forget this!" She was still uttering threats as they took her from the courtroom. John Kallinski showed no emotion whatever. He simply stood without looking at either Marcie or Kevin and allowed himself to be led away.

Marcie was stunned. Jeff reached for her and she fell into his arms, sobbing her heart out. Kevin was hugging her and patting her back. Finally, the tears subsided and Jeff whispered, "Come, Marcie, it's time to be on our way." She merely nodded and allowed herself and Kevin to be led outside. A car was waiting. The suitcases had already been picked up from the house and they left at once for the airport.

Chapter 15

The plane would be landing soon. She must wake Kevin. Marcie's fingers nervously clasped the ring suspended on the chain around her neck. She was filled with anxiety about meeting Jeff's parents. He had told her to put the ring on her finger before she got off the plane, but should she wait to meet Mr. and Mrs. Martin first. What if they didn't like her. *I know they'll like Kev; everybody falls in love with him, he's such a great little guy.* No, she thought, *I'll do just as he said, because they already know about our engagement.*

Before she and Kev boarded the plane, Jeff had told her that he and his parents had talked on the phone and he assured her they were looking forward to meeting her and having her and Kev stay with them until his transfer came through. She continued to stew. *What sort of people are they, to be willing to take a couple of strangers into their home!!! What am I thinking?* she said to herself. *They're Jeff's parents, they'll be just like him...sweet and understanding.* So she reached up and, unclasping the chain, removed the ring and slipped it on her finger. Reaching over, she gently shook Kevin's shoulder. "Wake up, Kev, we're almost there. The plane's preparing to land." He rubbed the sleep from his eyes and raised up to look out the window.

"WOW! Marcie, I can see the land coming closer and closer. I never seen anything like this *ever* before!" The couple across the aisle smiled at his enthusiasm. There was something Marcie had to do before they left the plane. She placed her left hand on

Kevin's. He looked down and, seeing the ring, sucked in his breath loudly then let it out with a whoosh. "'Where'd you get that beautiful ring, Marcie?" he whispered.

"Jeff gave it to me," she said, "we're going to be married when he gets his transfer back here. I didn't say anything before because it had to be a secret until we got to Oregon. But Jeff's parents know and I didn't want you to be in the dark if they should mention it when we meet them."

Kevin tried to whistle, but his front tooth was loose and all he made was a little shooshing sound. "It sure is pretty and sparkly," he said, "and...and... Marcie, us and Jeff being a family sounds really great!"

As the plane glided to a smooth landing, Marcie checked Kevin's appearance, smoothing his curls into place and patting out some of the wrinkles in his clothing. She should have let him wear the dungarees and tee shirt, she thought, they didn't wrinkle. *Oh, well, he looks fine. It's me that's a nervous wreck!!! I'm shaking so bad inside, I hope I don't get sick. Oh, my God, I've forgotten their names.* Jeff had told her to look for a middle-aged couple holding a sign with their first names written on it...suddenly she drew a mental blank..."Quick, Kevin," she said, "what are Jeff's parents' names? You know, the names on the sign they'll be holding. I've forgotten!"

Kev looked into her panic-stricken eyes. "Gee whiz, Marcie, you're gettin' awful forgetful these days. It's Josh and Alice. And, quit squeezin' my hand so tight, you're about to break all my fingers." With that remark, they both broke into laughter. Marcie knew then that whatever came up, she and Kev could face it together. So they prepared to leave the plane and begin yet another phase in their young lives.

Chapter 16

She held tightly to Kevin's hand as they entered the waiting area of the airport. Looking about, she spotted a rather tall woman with ash blonde hair set in a becoming style. At her side was a man with graying hair but a fit physique and several inches taller than her. As soon as their eyes met, the woman lifted a sign with *Josh and Alice* written on it. Marcie and Kevin walked slowly toward them and Alice broke into a big smile while Josh grinned, showing the laugh wrinkles at the corners of his eyes. Reaching out his hand, he said, "You must be Marcie and Kevin. Jeff told us to look for the best-looking people coming off the plane and you two certainly fit the bill." He took Marcie's hand and pulled her to him for a big hug. He then stooped and picked Kevin up in his arms as Alice took her turn at hugging Marcie. She, too, then turned to Kevin, giving him a big kiss on the cheek as he squirmed in embarrassment. "My dears, I know you must be worn completely out doing all this traveling. We're going directly home where Lucy has prepared us a nice lunch, then you're both going to take a long nap, because this evening Agnes and Corinne, they're Jeff's sisters, will be coming by with their families. They can't wait to meet the newest additions to the family. So, come along. We'll get your luggage and be on our way." Marcie smiled at her non-stop manner of speech and take-charge attitude. It was such a relief having someone else make the decisions. Marcie allowed Alice to take her arm and lead the way to the baggage pick-up. Josh, still carrying Kevin, followed.

The Martin home was situated in what appeared to be an older neighborhood, very nice and quiet with tree-lined streets. The car turned into a long driveway ending in a wide parking area in front of a three-car garage. A stepping stone walkway led to a corner porch that was screened in, holding white wicker furniture with bright cushions on the chairs and loveseat. A vase of fresh flowers set in the center of the table. The house was a two-story white frame home with green shutters at the windows. There was a welcoming atmosphere about the entire place. Marcie took Kevin's hand as they walked toward the porch. He began tugging at her hand.

"Look, look, Marcie," he said, "there's a great big back yard with a fence around it. We could have brought Puddles, she would have stayed in the yard." Remembering Puddles brought a feeling of sadness and homesickness over them both. Seeing the stricken looks on their faces, Alice quickly changed the subject by suggesting that later in the week they could take an outing over to the zoo, asking Kevin if he had ever seen monkeys and giraffes and other wild animals. He was soon intrigued by the impending trip and was chattering away with Alice.

They entered the house into a small entryway off the porch. Alice called out to Lucy and an older black woman appeared in the kitchen door. "Lucy, this is Marcie and Kevin," said Alice. "Marcie is going to be our new daughter as she and our Jeff will be getting married in a few months. Kevin is Marcie's young brother. She is his guardian and they'll be staying with us until after the wedding. Now, they are both hungry and tired and I promised you would have lunch ready for us."

"I'm very pleased to meet you both," said Lucy, bobbing her head, "and, yes, ma'am, lunch is ready. The weather is so nice I thought it might be pleasant to eat out on the porch. If that's alright with ya'll, then go right on out and have a seat and I'll begin serving." The table was soon filled with platters of chicken salad sandwiches, sliced cantaloupe and watermelon, and tall frosty glasses of iced tea. Soon after eating, Kevin began yawning.

"Uh oh," said Alice, "someone needs that promised nap. Let's go, kids, I'll show you to your rooms."

They went up the wide oaken staircase into the upper hall. Alice led them down the hall and entered a room on the right. "This will be your room, Marcie. You will notice it has twin beds. It used to be the girls' room when they were still at home. Kevin, you will be just across the hall in what used to be Jeff's room. Crawl into bed now and rest as long as you want. I see Josh has already put your suitcases in the rooms. When you awaken, you can refresh yourselves in the bathroom at the end of the hall; you'll share it. I'll leave you both now." Alice left them and went back downstairs.

Kevin looked at Marcie with big, scared eyes. "I don't want to stay across the hall by myself," he said. Marcie understood. Here they were, in a strange new part of the country, in the home of people they had just met…and…she hadn't mentioned this to Kevin, but the possibility of the mobsters finding them was always a threat.

"Come on, Kev," she said, putting her arm around his shoulders, "you can sleep in the other bed in here." She helped him take off his shoes and socks and, turning back the sheet and quilt, tucked him in. In a matter of moments, he was sound asleep. It wasn't as easy for Marcie to sleep, even though she was exhausted. As she lay in the comfortable bed, she looked around the cheery room they were in. White, ruffled, dimity curtains covered the double windows. The walls were painted in a mauve color and the quilt coverlets on the beds were in a mauve, peach and burgundy pattern of various flowers. Colorful rugs in the same shades lay beside each of the two beds. As Marcie enjoyed the pleasant and comfortable surroundings, her eyes began to droop and soon she, too, slept soundly.

Slowly, she awakened and became aware of where she was.

Opening her eyes, she looked across at the other bed. Kevin was still asleep. Marcie rose and, taking some clothing from her suitcase, walked down the hall to the bathroom. Stepping from the shower a short time later, she felt completely refreshed. She completed her toilette and pulled on a pair of light blue peddle pushers then a blouse with matching blue in the print. Her hair was still wet from the shampoo but she was able to comb the unruly curls back and pull them into a pony tail, fastening it in place with a blue plastic holder. Finished, she went back to the room to get Kevin up and prepare his clothes for his bath. Looking out the window, she realized by the coming dusk that they had slept all afternoon.

Kevin was chattering away to her as they made their way downstairs. He was dressed in his favorite dungarees, tee shirt, and sneakers. She heard voices coming from the front of the house so they headed in that direction. When they stepped into the living room, all faces turned toward them and the talking ceased. Marcie stared at the couple seated on the sofa, the young woman's hair was the same light brown as Jeff's and she had the same blue eyes. She jumped up and, coming forward with outstretched arms, said, "Marcie, I'm Jeff's sister, Agnes. It's so good to meet you." And, pulling Marcie into a hug, she continued, "This is my husband Les and that little scamp over there playing in the corner is our son, Carey. Let me just finish the introductions...Over here beside Dad is our sissy, Corrine, her husband, Joe, and the little sweetie on Grandpa's lap is Mindy. Everybody...this is Marcie, Jeff's 'intended.' Oh, let's not forget this other special person...Kevin." Standing between them, she put one arm around Marcie's waist and the other across Kevin's shoulders. Drawing them into the warmth of the family embrace, Agnes said, "Welcome, both of you."

Everyone jumped up and surrounded Marcie and Kevin and began hugging them and welcoming them to the family. Mindy was only three and she remained snuggled in her grandpa's arms, still shy around these strangers. Carey came over from where he had been playing in the corner with a stack of toy cowboys and Indians. He was a sturdy fellow of "almost six" as he put it. He offered to share his toys with Kevin and soon they were in the corner with a big cowboy and Indian battle going on. *It's as though we belong,* thought Marcie, and tears of happiness welled up, but she blinked them back and savored the moment. It was such fun listening to all of them reminisce about when they were kids and telling "tales" on Jeff, outlining his escapades. Agnes was the eldest, then Jeff, followed by Corrine. *Such a happy family,* thought Marcie, *and soon Kev and I will be a part of this.* She wanted to shout out loud...and, just before they went into the dining room for dinner, she stood and, facing them all, said, "I just want you all to know that I am overjoyed at the way you have welcomed Kevin and me into your family. You all are so kind and generous...just like Jeff. I know this goodness comes from the way you were raised by Josh and Alice. Kevin and I are so lucky!"

Alice came forward and, putting her arms around Marcie, said, "We knew you had to be special for Jeff to fall in love with you. We know also that life hasn't been easy but you both have stood up to the pressure. We are very proud to have you both in our family and I think it's a good idea for you to call us Mom and Dad. Since Jeff will probably adopt Kevin after your marriage, he can just call us Grandma and Grandpa starting right now!" Everyone cheered and, laughing, went in to dinner.

Shortly after dinner, Agnes and Corinne gathered their families and left. Alice and Josh sat talking quietly with Marcie. When the phone rang, Josh answered. It was Jeff. He spoke with his parents then asked for Kev, with whom he chatted for a few minutes. Then, it was Marcie's turn.

"Hello," she spoke breathlessly.

"Hi, sweetheart," replied Jeff. "I was saving the best for last. When I go to sleep tonight, I want to dream about you, so I want your voice to be fresh in my mind. How was the flight out? How do you like the family?"

Marcie told him about her nervousness before landing and the fact that she forgot his mom and dad's names. He laughed, but said it was understandable with all she had been through.

"I wanted to tell you that your dad was sentenced to ten years in prison with the possibility of parole in five years. His health is very poor, Marcie, so be prepared. He may not make it." Marcie was very still for a moment. It was almost like discussing a stranger, yet she did love her dad. He just hadn't been there for her for a long time.

"What about Lisa?" she asked.

Jeff continued, "It seems that she was the one responsible for their involvement with the racketeering. Her family had been involved over the years, and she took advantage of your father's accounting expertise and convinced him to join. Eventually, her greediness caused their downfall. She was sentenced to fifteen years, with parole possible after ten years. I'm real sorry, Marcie, especially about your dad."

Marcie cleared her throat and said, sorrowfully, "What they did was wrong. They'll have to accept their punishment. I don't want to think about them anymore. Maybe some day I can forgive them for what they have put Kevin and me through, but not right now."

Jeff happily changed the subject. "Well, sweetie, have you been making any wedding plans? I'm going to leave that up to you, but would like to schedule it within a day or two after I get there. I'll let you know the date just as soon as I get my transfer papers." There was a long pause and Marcie started to speak, when he interrupted her. "Marcie, sweetheart, I don't want to rush you into marriage. Please believe me, it's what I want with all my heart, but I realize you are very young and your life has been filled with turmoil. So, if you should change your mind between now and when I arrive, please know that, although it will hurt, I will understand."

"Oh, Jeff," Marcie cried, "I'll never change my mind. Spending the rest of my life with you is exactly what I want."

Then, she told him about Kev's comment when she showed him the ring and told him of their plans while still on the plane. "So," she said, "if anyone changes the plans, it will be you."

"Never," Jeff said gruffly.

Chapter 17

Jeff called at least once a week, sometimes twice. Marcie loved it when he called her "sweetheart." She wasn't aware that she was so starved for affection. Oh, Kev often hugged her neck and said, "I love you, Marcie," but she needed someone to share her thoughts and ideas. Someone to listen and care...to be a friend and companion.

She mentioned once that, perhaps, she should look for a job and contribute to the household, but Jeff insisted that he didn't want her to do anything that might leave a paper trail in the event "they" might be looking for her. "I have explained this to Dad and he agrees. You know, sweetheart, Dad is an attorney with a very large firm in Eugene; he can afford to feed the two of you, and, I'm sorry, it just didn't occur to me before this, but I'll speak to Dad and arrange for him to give you some spending money. I'll reimburse him later."

"No, no," Marcie interrupted. "Please don't do that. I have my savings that I withdrew from the bank before leaving Shelbyville. I don't need any money. Thanks anyway, but you'll start being responsible for us soon enough."

The months passed rather quickly. It was late in August and Marcie had taken Kevin to shop for school clothes. It was hard to believe that he would be entering school already. Alice had gone with them to the local elementary school to enroll him. She knew the principal, Mr. Harding, and had scheduled an appointment for Marcie to explain Kevin's background and the reason there was no valid birth certificate. It's true, Marcie could request a copy of his birth certificate from the Bureau of Vital Statistics in Kentucky, but this could possibly put them both in jeopardy. Alice assured Mr. Harding that once Jeff returned and he and Marcie were married, that Jeff intended to adopt Kevin and give him his name. "This will be done through the courts with the documents sealed. I realize it's asking you to bend the rules, but if Kevin could be enrolled as Kevin Martin from the beginning, it will be a lot safer for these young people. We have already taken him to our pediatrician for the necessary immunizations and this has been done under the name Martin." Apprised of this young boy's background, Mr. Harding agreed to enroll him as Kevin Martin. In fact, he prepared Kevin's file so that no one other than himself would have any knowledge of Kevin's unique situation. From that day forth, Kevin was referred to as Kevin Martin. He liked his new name and was thrilled that Jeff would be his "dad."

Finally, Jeff received his transfer papers. He called that evening to inform Marcie that he would be leaving D.C. on November 10th. He would be driving across the country and estimated that it would take him about four to five days to get there. "Oh, Jeff," Marcie screeched, "I can hardly wait! Wait till Kev hears." She was checking the calendar..."It'll be four weeks and either three or four days. Please drive carefully, but do hurry," she said. "How does November 18th sound as a wedding date?" she asked.

"I'm circling it on my calendar as we speak," Jeff replied. And so the wedding date was set.

The next time Jeff called, it was Marcie with some exciting news. She and Alice had been taking a walk through the neighborhood and, three blocks from his parents' home was a house for sale. It was empty and they went up to peek in the windows. Marcie grabbed a piece of scrap paper from her purse and quickly wrote down the realtor's number. It was too late that evening to call, but early the next morning she was on the phone making an appointment to see the place. She asked Alice to go with her and at 11:00 a.m. they met Mrs. Kravitz at the house. Marcie was crazy about the place. It was an older home situated on a large double lot. The back yard had several large trees and beautiful shrubs and flower beds...they needed to be trimmed, raked and mulched for winter. The front porch stretched across the entire front of the house. They entered into a good-sized foyer. On the right an archway led to the living room, with a huge bay window facing the front. On the left was a large formal dining room. Swinging doors led into a large eat-in kitchen, with all white wooden cupboards and butcher block counters. There were no appliances...but Marcie was thinking, *my table and chairs will fit in here nicely.* Beyond the kitchen was a utility room with hookup for a washer and dryer. Going back into the hallway, beyond the living room was another smaller room that could be used as a den. Oaken stairs with white painted railings led to the second floor. There were three bedrooms and two baths. The hardwood floors were in excellent condition. Marcie was thinking, *Oh, please, don't cost too much! I can see us living here...Jeff, Kev, and me!* Turning to Mrs. Kravitz, she said, "The most important question is how much is it?"

"Marcie," said Mrs. Kravitz, "this house has just gone on the market, but it's been empty for about three months because the couple who own it moved to San Diego to be near their children. They wanted to make sure they liked it down there before selling and just now decided to make the move permanent. Naturally, they would like to move it as quickly as possible, so it's practically a steal at $25,000. Marcie was totally ignorant of real estate prices, so she could only take Mrs. Kravitz' word that it was a "steal."

"I have to discuss this with my fiancé who is still on the East Coast. I expect him to call tonight. Can you not show it to anyone else until I can give you an answer tomorrow?" she asked.

"I'll mark it as a tentative purchase so no other agent will show it," she said. "But I will need to have an answer from you by noon tomorrow. Will that be enough time?"

Jeff was on the phone and Marcie was describing the place in as much detail as possible. "Hold on," he said, laughing, "you sound like you're the realtor."

"Oh, Jeff," she cried, "it's so perfect! Your mom was with me when we were able to go inside and she really liked it, too. When Dad came home this evening, we all went over and he walked around the outside and looked at the foundation and things like that. He thinks it is in good shape. And, he also thought the price was a 'steal.' But you need to tell me if you think we can afford to buy it. I still have some savings...after the cost of the wedding, I will be able to contribute $2,000 as a down payment. Do you think we can swing it? More importantly, do you trust me to make such a big decision without your seeing it? Kev said you and he would have to build a fence around the back yard so we can get another dog. He still misses Puddles. What do you think????"

Jeff said nothing for a few moments. It was making Marcie nervous. Finally he spoke and with a sound of awe in his voice said, "How did I ever find such a perfect person to be my wife? I know I didn't have this kind of common sense when I was eighteen. It sounds like a good deal and, of course I trust you to make a sound decision. Have Dad help you with the settlement. Any papers that need signing can be mailed to me here and I'll return them as quickly as possible. Also, give me the address. As soon as I get the papers and sign and return them to you, I'll have your furniture shipped directly to the house. We should be able to move in as soon as we return from our honeymoon...Oh, yes, *I* get to plan that part," he said, chuckling. He could almost see her blushing. "I got to go now," he began to whisper, "give me a kiss...hold the phone close to your lips, open your mouth slightly...bring the phone to your lips...that's it...can't you feel it, Marcie, I'm giving you a lover's kiss. Just three more weeks and it'll be the real thing. I can hardly wait...love ya, sweetie...bye!"

Marcie was breathless, her voice was shaking as she, too, whispered, "You're making me all tingly," and she giggled. " I love you, too, bye!"

Later that night, Kevin was in bed and Marcie went looking for Alice. She found her sitting in the living room working a crossword puzzle. "I need to speak with you about something personal," she said.

"Darling, you can speak to me about anything," replied Alice, laying the puzzle aside. Marcie was twisting the scarf that hung around her neck and looked very uncomfortable.

She finally blurted out, "Mom, I don't know anything about being a wife. There was never anyone to tell me. I was only seven when my real mom died and Lisa never got around to discussing anything beyond what to do when I began having my menstrual periods. Can you help me? Is there a book I can read, or something?" She looked so pathetic.

Alice took both her hands, saying, "Come, let's sit over here on the sofa. Dad's already gone upstairs so there will be no one to interrupt us." And thus Marcie received a sensitive enlightenment on what was expected of a wife in the marriage bed. Alice, having a kind and loving husband, was able to answer her questions candidly without embarrassment or leaving Marcie with any fear of the unexpected and unknown. She knew, too, that Jeff would be gentle with her.

Chapter 18

Between Mrs. Kravitz and Josh, all the necessary papers were signed and delivered, and on October 28th Marcie took possession of their home. Alice had a club meeting to attend that day; Kevin was in school so Marcie gathered up buckets, rags and cleaning supplies and went alone to her new home. It was so quiet in the house. She hadn't thought to bring a radio with her, so she went about her chores singing to herself. Suddenly, she had the strangest feeling. It was like someone was staring at her. She glanced quickly about then went to the front windows, but saw no one. She hurried to the front door and checked to make sure it was locked. Then she ran to the back door. It, too, was locked, but she couldn't shake that scary feeling. *I think I'd best go home*, she thought, and gathered her things hurriedly, placing them in the car. She left, looking around to see if anyone was following her, but she saw no one. The first thing she did when arriving at the Martins was contact a locksmith and arrange for all the locks to be changed on the outside doors of her new home. The next day she had the utilities turned on and a telephone installed. But she didn't go back to the house by herself anymore.

On November 4th she received a call from a transfer company saying they would be delivering a truckload of goods to 1412 Shady Lawn Avenue on Monday, November 7th and wanted to make sure someone would be there to receive the shipment. On Monday she and Alice prepared a thermos and some sandwiches and went to the house to await Marcie's furniture. It was almost noon when the truck pulled into the driveway. Marcie remembered when she and Kevin had received delivery of these items from the furniture store back in Shelbyville. The driver and his helper had placed all the pieces in the rooms where they belonged. Not so with these movers. With the exception of the beds and bureaus, which they did agree to carry upstairs, everything was set in the nearest space available, with the boxes of linens, etc piled wherever they found a spot. As soon as they left, Alice and Marcie pulled the table and chairs into the kitchen and proceeded to have lunch.

"Now," said Alice as soon as they had eaten, "let's get to the unpacking." By 4:00 o'clock they were both "pooped" out. All the dishes had been washed and placed in the cupboards; Alice had called her favorite appliance dealer and coerced him into sending someone out at once to install the washer and dryer. They washed and dried all the linens and put them away in the storage closets. They would have to wait until Dad could get Les and Joe to come help him put the beds together and carry the heavy items where Marcie wanted them placed. After dinner that evening, the fellows showed up along with Agnes and Corrine, who were anxious to see Marcie and Jeff's place. Everyone, including the kids, trouped over to Shady Lawn Avenue and, within a couple hours, furniture had been set in place throughout and, although it looked sparse in this large house, it was beginning to look like a home. Other than getting curtains and such for the windows, Marcie and Jeff together would pick out the remainder of furnishings that would be needed. She had selected the larger bedroom with connecting bath as her and Jeff's room. Kevin was allowed to choose which of the other two rooms he wanted as his bedroom. He picked the one looking out over the back yard. Marcie was glad that he seemed excited about settling into his new home with a room of his own. He still used the spare bed in Marcie's room at the Martin's and this had worried Marcie for some time.

Chapter 19

Jeff was expected home today! Marcie was alone. Josh was at his office as usual; it was Alice's day to volunteer at the local hospital and Kevin was in school. At about 2:30 Marcie was getting restless. She decided to take a short walk but intended to stay within sight of the house so she wouldn't miss Jeff's arrival, but was lost in thought and walked several blocks before she realized what she was doing. She looked at her watch. It was almost 3:00. Kevin's school bus would be dropping him off at 3:10, so Marcie turned to hurry back to the house. She was passing by an undeveloped lot with overgrown shrubs and trees, when a large black automobile pulled alongside of her and stopped. Quickly, a man dressed in black with dark glasses jumped from the front seat and grabbed her arm, saying, "Please get in the car, Miss Kallinski. Someone needs to talk with you." The back door opened and he shoved her into the car. Inside sat an older man dressed in an obviously expensive suit and he, too, wore dark glasses. It all happened so fast Marcie was unable to call out.

The man spoke, "We attempted to pick up your brother, Miss Kallinski, but the school guard was overzealous in her watchfulness." Marcie's heart began to beat frantically, but she said nothing. The man continued. "You're a very resourceful young lady. I wanted to meet you. I understand that a briefcase containing a very large amount of money was left in your possession but seems to have disappeared. What can you tell me about it?" Marcie knew definitely that she was dealing with the mob. She started to speak, but was so frightened all that came out was a squeak. She swallowed noisily. "Don't be frightened," said the man, "we mean you no harm. Take your time and tell me what happened to the briefcase."

Marcie cleared her throat. "It...it's just as I stated at my parents' trial. While my brother and I were traveling, it was left somewhere, but I can't remember where. You must understand that it was a time of great emotional upheaval in our lives. I didn't know where our parents were. I discovered by reading in the newspaper that our home was destroyed and I was suddenly faced with the responsibility for both my brother and myself. I was scared. In the beginning, I removed about $5,000 from the briefcase, which I used to purchase a used car, for the expenses of traveling, and for the furniture we needed when we decided to stay in Shelbyville, and other living expenses until I started receiving a pay check from my job. That's all I remember. When Kevin and I moved into the house in Shelbyville, I realized the briefcase was gone. When or where it was left is a total blank."

The man looked at her but she was unable to read his expression because of the dark glasses. "I believe you, Miss Kallinski," he finally said. "You're free to go. Your brother is probably worried about you. He should be home from school by now." Marcie realized they had been watching both Kevin and herself for sometime. That explained the eerie feeling she had experienced that day at the house on Shady Lawn.

"Yes," said Marcie, "he'll be scared." With that, the door was opened and Marcie stepped out.

The man spoke again. "Oh, yes, Agent Martin will be delayed a few hours. He experienced a bit of car trouble." With that, the door closed and the automobile sped away. Marcie took off running toward the Martin house. Kevin was just walking up the driveway. He turned around when he heard running footsteps.

"What's wrong, Marcie?" he asked. "Why are you running?" Marcie could see in his eyes the beginning of panic.

She quickly put her arm around his shoulders and said, "I was out for a walk and just realized it was time for you to be home from school so I ran to get here on time." She didn't want Kevin to worry, so said nothing to him about the incident. They had been home only about fifteen minutes when Alice returned from the hospital.

"Well, it looks like Jeff's trip is taking a little longer than he planned," she said. "He didn't call, did he?"

"No," Marcie replied. She hated the worried look on Alice's face and as soon as possible she made some excuse for Kevin to go upstairs. When he was out of earshot, she told Alice about the man in the car and what he had said about Jeff. For the first time, Marcie saw fear in Alice's eyes.

"I think I'd better call Josh," she said, and went quickly to the phone. She briefly retold the story to Josh who assured her that he was sure Jeff was fine and that he would leave immediately for home.

Shortly after Josh arrived home, the telephone rang. Marcie was standing next to it, so she picked it up. After her quick "hello" came Jeff's familiar, "Hey, sweetheart! How's my fav—" but got no further.

In a tear-filled voice, Marcie whispered, "Jeff, are you okay? Where are you?" then, she burst into sobs, unable to speak further.

Josh grabbed the phone from her. "Jeff," he said, "what's going on?" Jeff was stunned.

"Dad, what in the world is happening there? What's wrong with Marcie? Earlier today I had a little car trouble, which delayed me, but I'm just about an hour away now and wanted to let you all know. Now tell me what's wrong." Josh breathed a sigh of relief and told him what had occurred with Marcie and why she was so upset.

"Mostly it was relief at hearing you and knowing you were

ok," he said. "Just get in the car and hurry on in, Jeff, but don't speed and get careless," his dad said.

"I'm on my way," replied Jeff, "but first I'll make a quick call to the home office and see if I can get one of the agents to meet me at the house later tonight. See you soon. Tell Marcie everything is under control and she is to stop worrying."

Chapter 20

Marcie was in the bathroom holding a cold wash cloth to her eyes. Alice had given her some eye drops to remove the redness and now she was trying to get the puffiness to go down. How awful she would look when Jeff got there, she thought. She had showered and changed into a plaid skirt and soft white sweater. At least her hair was manageable today. She had allowed it to grow and it fell in soft waves to her shoulders. *I've done all I can do*, she said to herself, *so I will just go down and wait for Jeff.* Her heart began to flutter when she thought of being in his arms soon.

The entire family had gathered, the girls and their families as well. It had been almost two years since they last saw Jeff. They agreed that Marcie should be allowed to greet him first. A car was coming up the driveway. "Oh, Agnes," Marcie said, "are my eyes still puffy?"

"Don't worry about it," she said, laughing, "he won't notice anyway. Don't you know he's as nervous as you are about this meeting?" Marcie went out the back door, crossed the porch and stood on the stepping stone path leading to the parking area. Jeff's car stopped and he got out. His eyes were on Marcie and, as he came around the car, his arms opened wide and she flew into them. She was beginning to cry again. Her shoulders were shaking. Jeff held her close, rubbing her back and whispering words of comfort.

"Please don't cry, we're together now and everything is going to be fine." Finally she was under control and lifted her tear-stained face to him, managing a wobbly smile. Jeff spoke, "Hey, sweetheart, don't you think it's about time I got one of those passionate kisses we've been practicing all these months?" With his left hand under her chin, he lowered his mouth to hers for a long awaited kiss.

After several moments, a shout was heard from the back porch. "Marcie and Jeff, quit all that smooching. I want to hug Jeff and Grandma won't let me inna'rupt you guys!" With that, they broke apart, laughing, but Jeff's arm remained tightly around Marcie's waist, holding her close to him.

"Come on, big fella," he called, and Kev came bounding off the porch almost knocking him off his feet when he jumped, throwing his arms around his waist in a big hug. Jeff had his arms around both Marcie and Kev, smiling hugely.

"I almost forgot something important," Jeff said. "You two wait right here." He turned back to the car and, opening the door said, "OK, come on out and get reacquainted." Out jumped Puddles. She circled Jeff twice then spied Kevin. Immediately the two, child and dog, were down on the ground hugging and yapping. There was never a happier youngster than Kevin at that moment. Then, the rest of the family came trooping out and shouts of greetings, backslapping, hugging and kissing went on for several minutes.

A bell jingled, and Lucy stood on the back porch with a big smile, saying, "I spent all day preparing this feast for you, Mr. Jeff, now you get yourself and the rest of the family in this house and to the table before the food all spoils."

"Lucy, the best cook in the whole United States! I'm on my way!" He bounded up the walk and onto the porch, picking up Lucy in a big bear hug. She swatted at him with her dish towel, all the time with a big smile on her face. The family was complete again. They all trooped in and sat at the large dining room table. They had outgrown it, so Kevin and Carey sat at a small side table and Mindy was in her high chair next to Corrine. The succulent roast beef with all the trimmings was served and for the next hour the whole family talked non-stop, catching up on what was happening in each of their lives.

Finally, Jeff excused himself. He had to shower and change clothes after the long day of driving. He informed the family that Agent Marcus Denby was coming over later on and that they needed to discuss what had happened to Marcie earlier that day.

Later that evening Agent Denby and Jeff both listened to Marcie's story several times and they agreed that she must have spoken with Mitch DiChello. He was the "boss" in this area and her description fit him. Agent Denby said, "Let's play it cool for a while. I'm for taking the man at his word when he says he believes Marcie. We'll keep the group under surveillance for a few weeks in case they try to bother her again, but I truly believe they have decided to write off this loss and forget the whole deal. They really got their revenge when Marcie's parents were put in prison. Had there been any money to recover, that would have been icing on the cake. Not that we would have let them get their hands on it if it had been found by us. Who knows, the money may be molding away buried in a trash pile somewhere. Or, if some lucky soul found it, I hope he was poor and, by now, has divvied it up among all his family and friends and spent it well." Changing the subject, Marcus asked Jeff and Marcie when the wedding was to be.

"In three days," replied Jeff. "We'll get the blood tests and license tomorrow." Marcie screwed up her face in mock terror of having to have a blood test. "We haven't had time to go over plans entirely, but from our telephone conversations I understand it will be small. Just the immediate family and a few close friends." Looking at Marcie, he said, "We're still planning it for here at home, aren't we?"

"Yes," Marcie whispered, holding on to Jeff's hand and looking into his eyes adoringly.

"I think it's time to say goodnight," said Marcus and he took his leave.

Chapter 21

Flowers were everywhere. Garlands of pink miniature roses and white babies breath were entwined around the bannister of the stairway. The minister had taken his place near the fireplace, where the mantle was banked with a spray of white and pink roses. Various arrangements of pink and white flowers were placed throughout the room. Mrs. Winters from the church was at the piano, playing softly as family and friends took seats in borrowed folding chairs that had been placed in the living room. Jeff, dressed in a soft dove gray tux, entered from the library with his father, wearing a dark blue suit, at his side. They took their place at the minister's left and, at that moment, Mrs. Winters opened with the traditional wedding march. All eyes moved to the head of the stairs. There stood Marcie.

Her dress was tea length satin, cut in the princess line, trimmed with Belgium lace around the scoop neckline and delicate pointed wisps of the same lace dropped over her hands from the narrow sleeves. A short lacy mantilla served as her veil. Her satin pumps completed the ensemble. Her only jewelry consisted of the shiny gold chain that had held her engagement ring when Jeff first gave it to her. At her immediate right stood Kevin wearing a dark blue suit like his "grandpa" wore. He put out his left arm and Marcie placed her hand on it and they began the descent down the stairs and through the family and guests toward Jeff. Marcie's eyes glittered with happiness. Jeff's eyes never left her face. She was such a vision of loveliness. When they reached the appointed spot, the minister asked, "Who gives this bride in marriage?"

Kevin spoke up loudly and clearly, "I do!" He then placed Marcie's hand in Jeff's and stepped back and took a seat next to Alice. There were tears in the eyes of everyone in attendance.

The ceremony was brief, and at the conclusion Jeff gave Marcie a loving kiss, whispering, "I love you, Mrs. Martin. May you always be happy." She clung to him with eyes shining, unable to speak through the emotion that filled her. As they turned to face the congregation, everyone broke into applause for the happy couple. They then proceeded to the dining room for the reception. Lucy had "done herself proud" in preparing the food.

Someone said it was fit for a king, but Lucy said, "No, this is for the prince and princess." She had become as devoted to Marcie and Kevin as she was to the rest of the Martin family. Alice had arranged for the three-tiered wedding cake, which had white wedding bells on either side of the miniature bride and groom topping the cake. After all the well wishes and congratulations, Marcie, along with Agnes and Corrine to assist her, went upstairs to change clothes and prepare for the wedding trip.

Jeff had told Marcie to bring casual clothing for their trip...blue jeans, shirts, and walking shoes. For the leave-taking she chose mauve slacks with a matching sweater and brown loafers. Jeff took her suitcase and placed it in the car alongside his own. All the guests had left except family members and they gathered around to wish them fond farewells. Jeff had opened the car door for Marcie when, suddenly, Kevin rushed at her, throwing both arms around her waist and bursting into tears. "What'll I do if they come get me while you're gone?" he cried. "You won't know where to find me and I won't be able to live without you and Jeff...I'm scared, Marcie."

She stooped down and put her arms around the little boy, hugging him tight. Jeff, too, hunkered down beside them. Josh came over and, laying his hand on Kevin's head, he patted him and said, "You don't have to worry about a thing. Me and Grandma are going to move one of the half beds into our bedroom so we can watch over you. Jeff and Marcie will only be gone three days and as soon as they return you all are going to live in your own new place."

Marcie broke in, telling Kevin that while she was gone he could be thinking about how he wanted his room to be fixed up. "Your room will be the first one we do when we get back," she promised. Kevin sniffled a couple times and Josh pulled out his handkerchief and wiped his face.

He then picked him up and said, "Tell Jeff and Marcie to have a good time on their wedding trip, kiddo. You and me and Grandma will hold down the fort while they're gone." The young lad gulped a couple of times, then leaned over and hugged both Marcie and Jeff and told them he'd draw a picture of how he wanted his room to look and would see them in three days. With that, Marcie and Jeff were able to be on their way.

Chapter 22

They were so happy. Marcie snuggled up to Jeff's side as he drove. They turned the radio on and sang along with the McGuire Sisters and Bobby Darrin and other pop singers. After about forty-five minutes, Jeff turned off the main highway onto a gravel road, which they traveled for another half hour. Twilight had set in when he turned into a tree-lined drive leading up to a small cottage. By then they were both tired and hungry. They had been too excited to eat much at the reception. Jeff got out of the car and went over and opened the cottage door. He entered and turned on the lights before coming back to the car for Marcie and the luggage. Marcie entered the front door and was amazed at how charming it was inside. The main room was highlighted by a huge fireplace on one wall. The oversized sofa and chairs looked so comfortable. Maple side tables were placed strategically around the room with brass lamps. A large wood and brass wagon wheel chandelier overhead provided central lighting. Jeff carried their luggage into the larger of two bedrooms. The kitchen was bright and cheery with built-in cabinets of warm pine. A small table with four chairs set in the kitchen.

Jeff grabbed Marcie and said, "Quick, let's go out the back door and see if we can catch the sunset on the water." From the screened-in back porch, steps descended down to a boat dock about fifty feet away. With his arm about her shoulders, they stood in awe as the last rays of the sun glittered across the still waters of the lake. Marcie then shivered from the cold and they went back inside. Jeff lit a fire in the fireplace and Marcie went into the kitchen to see what food was available. Opening the refrigerator, she was surprised to see a ham, potato salad, baked beans, and sandwich buns, along with all the trimmings. A well-stocked refrigerator indeed, there was even ice cream for dessert in the freezer.

When Jeff approached his friends, Zeke and Addie Carpenter, about renting the cottage for a few days, Addie had insisted on stocking it with food as their wedding gift to the young couple. Marcie began setting food out on the table, first placing the beans and ham in the oven to heat. Within twenty minutes Jeff was slicing the ham while she prepared the sandwiches and spooned potato salad and baked beans onto two plates. Each decided to have a glass of milk with their supper. Rather than sit in the kitchen, they carried their plates into the living room in front of the fireplace to dine. They seldom lacked for conversation, but even the silences between them were companionable. Afterward, they shared the clean up chores and soon the kitchen was spotless again. Jeff tuned the radio to a station of pop/rock tunes and they began to dance around the room. As they danced a slow two-step, Jeff pulled Marcie closer and began to nuzzle her ear. She giggled and he stopped dancing...looking into her eyes as he continued to hold her close.

"Do you think it's too early to go to bed?" he asked huskily. A slight blush appeared on her cheeks as she slowly shook her head negatively.

Jeff indicated that Marcie should go ahead in the bath to get in her night clothes. When she came out, he had already turned out the lights in the rest of the cabin. Only the bedside lamps were lit. He sat on the edge of the bed dressed only in pajama bottoms. On the dresser set a tray with an ice bucket holding a bottle of champagne along with two silver-lipped champagne glasses. "A gift from Mom and Dad," Jeff indicated with a nod of his head.

"Oh, I've never tasted champagne before," said Marcie.

"I thought you probably hadn't. So you better limit yourself to only one glass. I wouldn't want you to get drunk and pass out on me," he said, laughing.

Marcie wore a white cotton batiste night gown, with delicate ruffles of lace around the neckline and cap sleeves. She hesitated shyly near the bathroom door and Jeff walked over and pulled her close, kissing her deeply. She wrapped her arms about his waist and melted against him. Gradually, the kiss ended and Jeff, breathing hard, picked her up and carried her to the bed.

The covers had already been turned back; he placed her in a sitting position and pulled up a pillow to prop her back. He then went to the dresser and poured the champagne. Bringing the drinks back to the bed, he sat down next to Marcie's knees and, handing her a glass, said, "A toast! To the smartest and most beautiful bride ever. Thank you for making me the happiest guy in the world. I wish only happiness for you." They touched glasses, and sipped the champagne.

Marcie then said, "I, too, have a toast! To the most loving, kind man in the world, who makes me feel so warm and safe. I love you with all my heart and want to spend the rest of my life making you happy." They again touched glasses and sipped the champagne. Marcie wrinkled her nose as the bubbles tickled it. They both laughed as the glasses were emptied. Jeff offered to refill them, but Marcie declined. She already could feel a happy buzz from the one glass.

He carried the glasses to the tray, returned to the bed and turned out the lights. As he crawled into the bed beside her, she moved into the circle of his arms and allowed him to kiss and caress her as lovers have done throughout the centuries, bringing her to heights of ecstasy, which she had never known. As she still lay trembling from the spasm of delight, Jeff whispered, "Marcie, it is possible for you to become pregnant from this first time. If you prefer to wait awhile before we plan a family, I will use a precaution. It's up to you."

She looked up at him and said, breathlessly, "Let's let nature decide when we start a family. I'm willing anytime it happens. Okay with you?" He covered her face with kisses, ending with her mouth as he entered her for the first time. It was painful and Marcie pulled back, but Jeff stilled his body and held her close and soon the hurt was over and shortly Jeff moaned and shuddered, then lay still. After a moment, he rolled over keeping her at his side. "Oh, sweetheart, you are perfect. I love you."

They lay holding each other close and soon the stirrings of desire began to build again. This time there was no pain for Marcie, only the delight. Later, as Jeff lay sleeping at her side, she curled closer to him, enjoying the faint scent of talcum on his body, and thinking what a lucky person she was to have someone so wonderful to love and be loved by. She then fell into a restful sleep.

She awoke to the smell of food. Marcie was ravenous. Jeff was already out of bed, so she grabbed her robe and headed for the bathroom. After showering and donning fresh clothing, she went into the kitchen, feeling shy about seeing Jeff this morning after the night of passion they had shared. He was whistling cheerfully as he fried bacon and eggs. Glancing up as she entered, he smiled. "Good morning, sweetheart." Coming over to her, he gave her a big hug and kiss. "Ready for breakfast? You can make the toast and pour orange juice. The eggs are just about done." Marcie got out cups for coffee as she noticed he had brewed a fresh pot. So they shared their first breakfast as a married couple.

The next three days were filled with nature hikes, a boat trip (but it was too chilly to stay out on the water very long), long hours talking about plans for their home and their future, and, of course, those tender moments of intimacy, which they shared often. Then, it was time to go home.

Chapter 23

As they had promised Kevin, his was the first room they fixed up. Josh and Alice had gone into their attic and brought down a wooden toy box that had belonged to Jeff. It was included in the drawing Kev had made to show them how he wanted his room arranged. As the first night approached for them to stay in their home, Marcie secretly worried as to whether Kevin would balk at staying in his room by himself. But, there was no problem. It seemed that all he needed was the reassuring presence of Jeff being in the house. As bedtime approached, he bade them goodnight and scampered off to his room with Puddles at his heels and old teddy in his arms. Next morning, Marcie walked him to the corner to wait for the school bus. Jeff had the rest of the week off, so they went to town to make some additional furniture purchases for their home.

Chapter 24

Their first Christmas together was exciting. The three of them went out a few days before Christmas Eve to select a tree. Snow was falling lightly and they scampered gleefully throughout the lot in order to find just the right one. Before going home, they stopped by the variety store to buy lights, bulbs, tinsel and other decorating items. Marcie had a few ornaments from their days in Shelbyville, but not near enough for the huge tree they had purchased. She was looking longingly at a large decorated wreath of fresh greenery, thinking how lovely it would look on the front door, but the price was pretty high. Jeff saw the look on her face and, coming up beside her, said, "If you want it, buy it. I can read your thoughts and agree it would really brighten up the front door."

Marcie punched him and laughingly said, "How do you do that? Always knowing what I'm thinking!" He just grinned down at her, lovingly. It was a little past Kevin's bedtime before they had put the final touches to the tree. After turning on the colored lights, they all three stood back and oohed and aahed and agreed it was the best tree ever.

Christmas morning they were up bright and early. Santa had left a shiny new bicycle for Kevin, along with items of clothing and a few games. Jeff gave Marcie a string of pearls and a lovely dress of light blue, which the pearls complimented nicely. Jeff received a pair of charcoal gray slacks and a light blue pullover sweater with matching shirt and tie. Kevin had made each of them a picture he had drawn in art class at school, as well as a silhouette of himself that had been done at school as a surprise for all the parents. Later, they gathered the gifts they had for the other family members and walked the few blocks to Josh and Alice's where the entire family was gathering for Christmas dinner.

The weeks passed by…It was Valentine's Day and Marcie had baked a cake in the shape of a heart and was decorating it. She had made a card for Jeff. After supper, she brought out the cake for dessert and presented a valentine card to Kevin, then handed Jeff his. He opened it and read…ROSES ARE RED, VIOLETS ARE BLUE, SOMEONE'S GOING TO BE A DADDY IN SEPTEMBER, CAN YOU GUESS WHO? His eyes widened and he looked at Marcie for several minutes before saying, "Are you sure?"

"Dr. Webster confirmed it today," she said. With a whoop, he was around the table, pulling her into his arms, raining kisses all over her face and then picking her up in his arms he began swinging her around.

Kevin looked at them like they were crazy. "What's wrong with you guys?" he finally asked. They happily explained that in a few months, a little baby would be coming to live with them. He had to think about it awhile…after all, other than little Mindy, he hadn't been around any babies and didn't really know much about them…but, seeing how happy Marcie and Jeff were he assumed it must be a good thing that was about to happen to them. And so they all began to look forward to the arrival of the little bundle of joy.

Chapter 25

September 1959

Jeff pulled into the driveway and parked the car. From the seat beside him he picked up a gaily-wrapped package. As he unlocked the front door and entered the house, he heard laughter emanating from the kitchen and made his way to his family. Marcie was at the table putting final touches on a birthday cake. A single large candle in the shape of the numeral one was ready to go in the center. Deanna Alice, named after Jeff's mother and Marcie's late mother, was seated in her high chair waving a spoon around that had been dipped in chocolate cake batter. She had it smeared on her face and even a glob in her hair. She proceeded to start banging it on the tray of her chair, causing batter to fly everywhere. Marcie immediately grabbed the tiny hand and removed the messy spoon.

Deanie, as she was called, shrieked in unintelligible baby jargon, her displeasure at having the spoon removed. "Hush, Deanie," said Marcie. "Be a nice little girl. Daddy will be here soon and we don't want a messy kitchen for him to have to look at."

The tiny girl with light brown curls and blue eyes like her daddy, blinked at her mother and said, "Dada!"

Marcie squealed. It was the first time Deanie had said Dada so plainly. Kevin was seated at the other end of the table doing his homework and he, too, looked up, wide eyed at his little sister's words. At that point, Jeff peeked around the doorway, saying, "Hey, I thought you were supposed to get presents today, instead you're giving us presents by learning how to talk."

"Hi, Munchkin," he said as he kissed the rosy cheek, trying to avoid the chocolate. She tried to grab him, but Marcie intervened with a damp cloth to wipe clear the mess from both hands and face of the child. Jeff then picked her up, turned to kiss Marcie and tousled Kev's hair.

"How's my birthday girl?" he said. "Got a kiss for daddy?" Deanie hugged his neck with her chubby little arms and planted slobbery kisses on his cheek. Jeff beamed. After dinner, they all had birthday cake and Deanie was given her birthday presents and allowed to rip off the wrappings. The paper and ribbons proved to be as fascinating as what was wrapped in them.

Later that evening, Kevin had gone to his room and Deanie was in bed for the night. Jeff was reading the evening paper when Marcie came in the den and sat on the arm of his chair. He noted the slightly troubled look in her eye, so he laid the paper aside and pulled her down onto his lap, saying, "What's your problem, sweetie? Tell me and I'll make it go away."

She snuggled close to him and said, "I need to talk with you privately, up in our room." It was getting late so he set her on her feet and went about closing up the house for the night. They then made their way upstairs. In their bedroom, Jeff sat on the bed, leaning back against the headboard. Marcie sat down and said, "Jeff, do you think you earn enough money that we could put $500 in savings each birthday for both Deanie and Kevin?" He looked at her quizzically.

"Oh, it might strap us a little, but we could probably do it. Why do you ask?" he said. He could see her sigh of relief and wondered what was to come next. "Well, I opened an account today for Deanie and would like to do the same for Kevin even though his birthday was last month."

"Where did you get that kind of money, Marcie?" Jeff questioned. She rose from the bed, went to the closet and from the top shelf pulled out a large Modess box, yellowed a little with age and dust. Bringing it to the bed, she opened it up and proceeded to pull out wrapped bundles of money...$100's, $50's and $20's. Jeff's mouth fell agape and he stared at her; then he fell over on the bed and began to laugh. He laughed so hard there were tears running from his eyes. "Oh, Marcie," he cried, pulling her down beside him, "you never cease to amaze me. A young girl, forced by her family to assume the role of adulthood, has duped us all, her family, the mob, and the agency. How did you do it without committing perjury at the trial of your parents?"

"But, Jeff," she replied, "no one ever asked me where the *money* was. They just kept harping on and on about the *briefcase*. That I did lose. I still cannot tell you where it was left. The first day Kevin and I were on our own I removed $5,000 from the case. From that, I bought the car and later paid our expenses while in Shelbyville until I started collecting my payday from the clothes pin factory. All the rest of the money was put in this box and stayed there until we bought our home. Then I took out $2,000 to help with the down payment. I wasn't truthful with you about the $2,000. I implied it came from my savings. I'm so sorry. I've never lied to you about anything else, not ever. Otherwise, I used my savings from when I worked plus the money for the car that was sold. Today I took out $500 for Deanie's savings account. I thought if I kept putting it in savings each year for the kids, one day it would all be in the bank. If we have more babies we'll treat them all equally.

"Also, I've been thinking about my dad. When he gets out of prison maybe we can use some of this to help him. I'm beginning to forgive him for his weaknesses. I guess I feel that way because, if it hadn't been for his and Lisa's actions, I never would have met you and that has, by far, been the most wonderful thing that ever happened to me. I started worrying this afternoon after I deposited the money for Deanie that maybe the bank would investigate you for having more money than you earn. Oh, Jeff, I don't ever want this money to cause you any trouble. Please tell me what to do!" She curled up beside Jeff, putting her arms around his waist. He was still chuckling but held her close and started thinking about what the ramifications could be if it became known that the money was in Marcie's possession.

After a few moments he sat up and, looking at Marcie, said, "It's wrong for us to use this money. To even things up between the two kids, we'll open an account for Kevin tomorrow with $500. But that's the end of it." He methodically began picking up the bundles of money and replacing it in the box. He was thinking about what she had said about her dad. He was glad to hear her say she was forgiving him. Jeff kept abreast of what was happening to both John and Lisa. John's health was poor and he gave no one any trouble at the prison. He would be eligible for a parole hearing next June and it was possible that he could be released.

Jeff decided the money would stay in the box on the shelf until John was out. He said to Marcie, "When your dad is released from prison, I'm going to take you to him. It's time for you two to become reconciled. We'll tell John that we will send him money each month to assist him but that money will actually come from this box. Never tell him or anyone about the money, Marcie. If it was known that this money existed, all of us would be in trouble. I can understand why you kept it. It was a safety net for you and Kevin. But others would be skeptical and your credibility would be questioned. We can't tell your dad because he might inadvertently let it be known to Lisa, although, I have been told that he has obtained a divorce from her."

Marcie was shocked. She had never asked about her dad and had no idea that Jeff had all this information concerning him. "Oh, Jeff," she cried, "I had no idea Daddy had divorced Lisa, but I'm glad he did. I'd like to go visit him but it's too far to travel. If you can get an address for me, I want to write to him. But I promise there will never be any mention of this money. Only you and I will ever know about the 'safety net.'"

Printed in the United States
32536LVS00009B/276